Crosses

&

Silver Bullets

Love and Conflict

Franklin Webb

crossessilverbullets@gmail.com

Illustrations by

Tyron Grice

https://tedwurx.myporttfolio.com

Only in love are unity and duality not in conflict.

R. Tagore

Seriously dude…have you ever read a love story?

Sage, Techno-alchemist

Crosses & Silver Bullets

Love in Conflict ©

Franklin Webb

1

Hey…it's you.

You actually waited twelve years?

Good.

A lot has happened…things change. People change.

What? Oh…Danion and Rail.

Like I said...things change…people change but I gotta tell you out of all the ways I thought this thing could end what did happened was something I really wasn't--- Whoa...don't want to spoil things here. After twelve year you deserved to know how this fairy tale ends.

Welcome to the Canadian Rockies where the sun has started it's early morning shift by lighting up the surrounding area of forest land. The sight of such a landscape brings two immediate things to mind. 1…beautiful as you see the work of Mother Nature and 2…as you see the cool air frosting over your own breath, 'Damn…it's cold!!'.

The acres of centuries old trees covered the land like an army standing at attention, but like with all armies' soldiers must fall and many did with one word.

"Timber!" the lumberjack yelled as the 70-foot tree came crashing down to earth.

"No one says 'Timber' anymore Dave." yelled the foreman John.

"Hey…that's half the fun of the job."

"Our job is clearing the way for that building site and with the money they're paying us we are gonna be on time."

"Yeah…what they're paying us." Dave said in a suspicious tone.

"What…you're complaining?"

"Hell no, Chief, but when have you ever known a big-ass company to pay three times what a job's worth?"

"Said they needed it done in a hurry." said John.

"Or…just needed it done. Two other crews before us…remember?

"Don't start."

"Talked to a couple of 'em. Weird shit boss man."

"Like…?"

"Brand new equipment breaking down."

"Sabotage. Two words..." John said. "Tree huggers."

"Spooky lights"

"Spooky lights?" the foreman chuckled. "I'll call Scully and Mulder"

"Well laugh at this…three guys got attacked by a bear."

John's smile went away.

"Okay…that I did hear about." he said. "But it was probably a rogue grizzly."

"Hasn't been a grizzly seen in these parts for years and the first one attacks three lumberjacks?" asked Dave.

"Well, I don't know…we're in the forest, they're in the forest, we just might run into each other." said John. "Listen…if you're worried about a bear attack...don't be they said they got the thing last week."

"Oh...yeah and they wouldn't lie to keep things on schedule."

"You saying the bear still out here?"

"You see it?"

"What?"

"The bear?" asked Dave. "Did you see the 'quote unquote' bear they 'got'?"

"Well...no."

Dave rolled his eyes making his point.

"Hey...do you really think I put this crew in danger if I honestly thought there was a rogue bear out here?"

"I just hope it is a bear." Dave said under his breath.

"What?"

"Nothing."

"What?" John demanded.

Dave thought about it and reluctantly told his foreman what was on his mind.

"My old man was lumberjack, Grandpa too, hell…most of my family's been doing the job for who knows how long." Dave said. "So…a few things get passed down. Stories."

"Like?"

"Like forest...spirits. Guardians who don't like people trumping on their land so they fight back."

"And that's what you think happened to the last crews?"

"Not saying that but---"

"Fairies?!" cried John.

Immediately the other men looked at John and Dave. The two quickly shrugged their shoulders in a masculine way since they both know as lumberjacks the word 'Fairie' shouldn't be in their vocabulary.

"I've heard those stories too." said John. "When I was five and my grandmother was reading me a bedtime story. Now if you don't like this job and the money that goes with it I suggest you start a new career writing fairy tales. Me…I'm gonna pay for my kid's braces by going to the other hill and surveying the next site of trees. Oh...and if I see anything 'spooky' I'll let you know."

With a laugh and a shake of his head John headed through the army of trees to the top of the hill. Down to his right he saw his crew clearing away the fallen trees and to his left the next section of trees to be cut down. As he looked at the landscape he was quickly reminded how beautiful it was out there. He took a deep breath and could easily see why the 'tree huggers' fought so hard to keep the forest standing but they didn't have a wife, two kids, and a mortgage to pay off.

"Breath taking isn't it?" a woman voice said to him.

"Yeah…I--- What?"

He turned around and saw the most beautiful woman with milky white skin and wavy long blond hair that had a green-leaf reef around it. Her eyes were a deep sparking blue that instantly drew you in closer to her smile. She seemed to glide upon the ground as she past John to get a better view of the forest. The dress she was wearing was a shear thin silk one-piece that when the light hit just right you could see the silhouette of her very fit body. John quickly had to remind himself 'Wife and two kids. Wife and two kids'.

"Amazing isn't it?" she said. "This place has survived floods, fire, pollution, and yet the one thing that can help this land most is its greatest threat."

'Ooh…great.' John unhappily thought to himself. 'A tree hugger.'

Who wasn't wearing any shoes he suddenly noticed.

"Who are you?" he asked curious about her.

"Well that depends…are you really going to cut down all these trees?"

"Yeah." he plainly said having a job to do.

"Then in that case…I'm your worst nightmare!" she turned showing her disappointment to him with sunken black eyes.

Her smooth skin suddenly turned to an ugly ash-gray with deformed claws for hands. Her welcoming smile now had razor-shape teeth with a serpent's fork-tongue lashing out at John. The next sounds were the foreman's screams echoing through the forest. It was quickly followed by numerous others from his crew at the lumber site.

It was close to 9:00 in the P.M. when 8-year-old Sara called out to her baby-sitter.

"CJ…CJ!"

"What? You're supposed to be asleep." a young woman said coming into Sara's room.

"Her dark hair had grown pass her shoulders but she kept it in check by tying the back of it into a ponytail. The red and purple highlighted streaks were gone as well as a lot of her piercings. The ears were the only thing that still had earrings in them. There was a maturity in her which came from more experience than of age. It showed in her eyes…her Caribbean blue eyes.

Rail.

Well…Jordan now. It was her middle name. After a decade and two years she still hated her first name and would still kick your ass if you called her by it. Everyone who knew her called her Jordan or J. CJ she gave special privilege to Sara and a few other preteens. No adult called her this because she didn't want any association with that blond from that 'lifeguard' show.

"I want a story." Sara said.

"What kind of story?"

"A love story."

"A love story?"

"A true one."

"A true love story huh?" said Jordan.

She searched her mind to make up a story that was 'true' when she suddenly decided…she didn't know why to tell Sara a true love story.

"Once upon a time there was a prince... a handsome prince who could fly. And one night he saved the life of a very beautiful princess and they fell in love. Each night he would take her in his arms and they would fly into the air where no one could hurt them. But the prince and the princess came from two different kingdoms that hated each other and didn't want them together. So much so that the princess' grandmother and the prince's…'friends' worked together to break them up."

"How?"

"An evil bit…'witch' gave the grandmother a potion to make the princess sleep and make the prince think she was dead. When he thought the princess was dead the prince broke down crying and decided to kill himself."

"Like Romeo and Juliet." said Sara.

"Just about."

"That had a sad ending I want a happy one."

"A happy ending huh?" Jordan said also wanting one for this familiar tale. "Okay…the potion was supposed to last for three days but it wore off in one. The princess found out about the evil plot and hurried to tell the prince she was still alive…"

Jordan paused remembering what actually did happen when she went to tell Danion she was still alive. The memory was close to bringing tears but she sucked it up to finish the story.

"…She hurried to tell the prince she was still alive and stopped him from killing himself…she made it just in time. They hugged and kissed then flew away from the two kingdoms and their hate living happily-ever-after."

"That's it?" Sara asked wanting more.

"No…they had a little princess of their own who knew when it was time to go to sleep." said Jordan. "Like now."

She tucked Sara in and kissed her on the forehead 'Good-night'.

"CJ…did that story really happen?"

"It should have…now 'Good-night'."

An hour went by as Jordan quietly watched TV then heard three voices approaching from down the apartment building hallway. When the door opened two men and a woman walked inside vocally expressing their enjoyment of the day.

"Shhh." Jordan said. "I'm trying to beat the limit of an hour were I actually think she'll stay asleep."

"Sorry." Sara's mother Claire said. "So…how was your day with the terror?"

"It was fun."

"Spoken like someone who wasn't at the toy store last week." Claire joked. "Thank-you. Since Sara, me and Robbie haven't gotten out in...ever and just to have the whole day where we didn't have to do the parent thing..."

"I bet."

"Mommy? Daddy?" Sara called from her bedroom.

"Almost made it." Claire said tapping on her watch. "I'll go."

"No…relax. I'll go." Claire's husband Robert said kissing his wife then heading for his daughter's room. "Hey sunshine isn't someone supposed to be sleeping?"

Giggling came out of Sara as her father went in her room to check and tuck her in again with Claire smiling proudly over her attentive husband.

"My man." Claire gleamed. "Coffee?"

"Sure." said Jordan

They headed to the kitchen and put four cups of water in the microwave.

"So…how did things go this morning?"

"Didn't know what hit them." said Claire.

"I hope so."

"Don't worry the OC made them forget. All those green killers will remember is that they were attack. By whom or what they won't be exactly sure but the fear of the experience will definitely keep them very far away."

"Till the next crew comes along."

Probably…but with each delay James loses money." said Claire. "So maybe if there are enough delays he'll move his precious building site someplace else."

"Don't bet on it." said Jordan. "People like James don't give up on things they really want and someone with his money can afford to take care of any problems and not worry about the consequences. Especially when you're dealing with something that's not supposed to exist."

"Sounds like the voice of experience." said Claire.

"Once or twice." replied Jordan. "But that's water under the bridge. If you two want to go out again I'll watch Sara anytime."

"You don't have to do that?"

"No…I want to."

"Great I'll repay the favor... hopefully very soon." Claire said pointing at Jordan's stomach with a raised eyebrow. "That is when the right guy comes around…or maybe he already has?"

Claire looked over to the young man that came in with her and her husband. His name was Craig Matters and Jordan knew exactly what was going through her friend's mind.

Mrs. Jordan Matters.

"Put the wedding bells away." said Jordan. "Craig and I are just friends."

"So were me and Robbie and in two months it will be our tenth anniversary."

"Time to go." Jordan said.

"What about the coffee?"

"Tomorrow…breakfast?"

"No prob." said Claire. Craig…J is leaving. Walk her home would ya?"

"Really doubt anything's gonna happen between here and down the hall." Jordan said knowing full well what Claire was up to.

"No...I have to get home myself. Tell Rob I'll catch him tomorrow." Craig said to Claire.

"Okay…good-night you two." Claire smiled hoping something could happen between her two friends while they were walking down the hall.

Jordan gave a subtle look of 'Don't start' to Claire as Craig opened the front door for her. As Jordan passed him to leave Claire gave a not-so-subtle look of encouragement to Craig about Jordan.

If you haven't guess it yet Claire, Robert, and Craig were all werewolves but not Howlers like Jordan. Their pack was known as the Gur-Fanng. A rather peaceful group compared to the Howlers, were they didn't have any continuous strife with any vampire caste but that didn't mean they like them either.

The old hate was still there.

Unlike Howlers Gur-Fanng preferred small towns to big cities which was one reason they didn't have much contact with vampires. These small towns were usually surrounded by large forest area. The Gur-Fanng believed that with the pack the forest gave their strength. Thus…they were very protective of it. All Gur-Fanng were environmentally friendly. Some were environmentalist others were Eco-terrorist but all would do what was necessary to protect mother nature…earning them the hated nickname 'Green-fang'.

"Well…she's not obvious." Craig said slightly embarrassed. "Sorry."

"Sal…" snickered Jordan.

""Who?"

"Old friend I haven't seen in a while, Claire reminds me of her."

"Where she now?"

"Last time I saw her was Reno 6 years ago. I really gotta call her up and find out how she's doing. Here's me..." Jordan said stopping at her apartment door.

"So...Rob's and Claire's tenth in two months."

Jordan looked at Craig wondering why he mentioned that from out of the blue. He responded by pointing to his ears in saying he heard her and Claire talking.

The anniversary not being the only thing.

"We'll probably have an early bash so they can be 'alone' later." said Craig.

"Be careful...if Claire has it her way she'll have us in engaged by the end of the party." Jordan said opening her door.

"Engaged...I think we should actually go on a date first. "he said. "Like Wednesday... to a movie?"

Jordan looked at Craig who was waiting for an answer hoping it would be 'Yes'.

"Craig..." she said taking a deep breath. "When I first got here you were one of the first people who really made me feel like I was welcomed and belonged by being a really good friend...who I really want to keep as a friend."

The old 'Just wanna be friends' speech. He knew that it was coming after that pause. It cuts to the quick doesn't it guys…but Craig accepted it.

"Okay" he said with some disappointment.

"Okay?" she asked seeing his disappointment.

"Okay." he assured her.

He started to leave but Jordan grabbed his arm to tell him something.

"One day a girl's gonna come along and she is gonna be so lucky to have you." she said kissing him on the cheek to assure him that it would happen. "Goodnight."

She closed the door behind her thinking it would be a little awkward the next time she saw Craig but was sure that things would be okay between them. Jordan's roommate however wasn't about to stay quiet about things.

"Tell me I didn't hear what I thought I heard." said Kefflynn.

"You were listening?"

A small light came flying up to Jordan's face in the form of a seven-inch fairie. She looked a lot like Jordan did 12 years ago with her short black. Her eyes were a dark brown with only two piercings in each ear with a small bracelet on her left arm. It was late so she was dressed for bed in a doll-size boxer shorts and hockey jersey cut in the back so her wings could flap free.

"How could I have not." said Keff. "Get back out there and tell Craig 'Yes! I would love to go out with you'."

"Don't start."

"Hey…that's prime man-candy getting away and a nice guy to boot. Why aren't you going with him.?"

"Cause we're just friends."

"What we have here is the classic tale of the handsome---I say again 'handsome' hometown boy who every girl wants in their bed---"

"Pleaze…Craig deserves better than a girl who just wants to jump him for the night."

"Yeah good thing he only wants one girl to jump him…and for more than just one night."

Kefflynn looked at Jordan clearly telling in silence who that 'girl' was but Jordan shook her head and walked by Keff to end the conversation.

"Can I ask you a question?" said Keff.

"If I say 'No' will it stop you?"

"Probably not." Keff said flying towards Jordan. "Do you want kids?"

"I guess…someday…maybe."

The question threw Jordan a little not really prepared to give an answer but Keff knew it.

"'I guess?' Someday?'" said Keff. "Who's the one who always volunteering to watch the kids during the OC and Gur-Fanng meeting? You. Who's always happy to babysit Sara? You. And who actually organized a baby shower last year? Oh… yeah you really don't want kids."

"So I like kids…doesn't mean I want an entire litter of them anytime soon. Right now I like kids for the same reason a lot of people do...they're not mine."

A reasonable answer but Kefflynn was persistent.

"Mom. Mom." she said to Jordan's stomach pretending to be the voice of a hopeful newborn. "I want out. I wanna play but I need a daddy first. Craig's a nice guy. Cute too. Which means I won't be ugly. That's a good thing."

"Good-night Keff." Jordan said quickly trying to get to her bedroom before Kefflynn could break into a song of 'Hush little baby'.

"One day you're gonna tell me about him."

"Who?"

"The guy you're still obviously holding a torch for for so long." said Keff. "How long as it been anyway?"

"12 years."

"12 years?" grasped Kefflynn. "Oh honey the torch has burned out. Move on and stop thinking about the one who got away."

"He didn't get away Keff...he died."

Immediately Kefflynn knocked herself in the head for being so stupid in pushing Jordan.

"J... I'm sorry." she said. "Do you wanna talk about it."

"No." Jordan clearly stated. "Thanks but...no. Goodnight."

Jordan went into her room and stripped out of her clothes. The tattoos from her Breaker days were all gone replaced with new ones. They were more spiritual in their designs and much more patterned across her body then her earlier ones. One stretched across the small of her back while two matching tattoos stretched down her thighs. It was the same with the tattoos on her shoulders they went down passed the top of her arms but still the Howler inside demanded some rebellion with a small tattoo surrounding her pierced belly-button. The last tattoo was on her right wrist in the shape of a bracelet. There were designs across it but they were used to hide a message in the tattoo. Jordan regularly covered it up with a wide watch band just in case someone got a good look and figured it out.

She put on her sweat shirt and shorts for bed and looked out the window to the small town of Jackson Point her home for the last four years. If you would have told her this was where she was going to be 12 years ago 'Rail' would have laughed in your face. Actually…she probably would have laughed and said 'Fuck-you'. A small town with just under a million people in it, adopted into a new pack, a fairie for a roommate, and baby-sitting and baby showering? 12 years does change a person but all in all things were not bad. A nice town with good friends and people. Yet…as she looked up into the night sky and caressing her bracelet tattoo she wondered if she trade it all to be up there again.

Flying…with him holding her in his arms.

Hell, the question was a moot one. He was gone. She accepted it…not really but who ever does completely? After 12 years she was still in love as she kissed her bracelet tattoo in a sense kissing him.

"Good-night Danion." she said heading to bed.

"She closed her eyes slightly hoping that she dream of him that night with no clue that soon the real thing would be back from the dead...but was that going to be a good thing?

Derrick James.

Millionaire. Multi-Millionaire.

Inherited his first million at the age of 15. After that he wisely invested in the stock market and the next new coming thing. Then came the internet and day-trading and the next thing you know his face was plastered on the cover of Forbes Magazine...twice.

Through his career he's had many goals one...to be rich and powerful. Achieved. Two...to make love to many beautiful super-models (every man's dream), and three...to build his own personal Camelot. A Zanado. A central point where he could control his entire corporate empire and show the world his greatness and massive ego.

Many architects were commissioned to design and redesign for the specifications of his dream and in three years it was a reality...on the blueprints. There was still one last thing. Location. Location. Location....and he found it six months ago while flying vie a private helicopter over the beautiful forest lands next to a no nothing town called Jackson Point. For the fulfillment of the dream and to make sure things were done the right way...meaning his way, James actually lowered himself to renting an upper-middle class house that was outside of town and away from the locals. His money and connections got him the land pretty quickly. All the permits and construction crews were ready. Finding a logging company that would clear the way for the groundbreaking was even easier. All that was needed was to cut down a few acres of hundred-year-old trees. The problem was these trees just happened to be on the land of the OC.

The OC

Short for Oberon's children. Yes…the king of the Fairies does exist but Shakespeare was half right. Oberon's not just king of the fairies but elves, gnomes, and all form of wood spirits. The OC actually do get their power from the forest that's why they're so protective of it. Using magic and trickery to 'discourage' woodsmen and settlers was easy in the old days but over the years they've slowly been losing their lands thanks to the demand of space from a growing human population and the advancement of logging equipment. Good thing they have an ally in the Gur-Fanng for nearly 300 years to get nasty in protecting the forest when humans approach a little too close…and this protection was costing James money and patience. He knew that he was going to have trouble with the OC and the Gur-Fanng. Yes…he knew about the fairies and the werewolves. James knew about the entire Lore society…he did business with a few them. In fact…he even had one in his employment.

Any guesses to who?

"Good to have you back Danion." said James. "So…how did it go in Brazil?"

"It took a little 'convincing' but there won't be any more hold ups on their side."

"Excellent. I'm sure Davis has told you about our current situation."

Fairies and werewolves. Not unexpected in this area and with what you're doing..."

"Neither here or there. You agree with the solution?"

"A bit extreme but it will get the job done." said Danion.

"I'm sensing some hesitation on your part."

"No…I'm just thinking why are you going through all this trouble when it would be easier to move your building somewhere else."

"On that point, sir. The cost effectiveness of simply buying a building and remodeling it to you sp----"

"Shut-up Davis." James told his 5-foot '3 balding tax attorney and financier. "Let me tell you Danion…at last check I was well worth over 125,000,000 dollars."

"125,578,232 to be exact." said Davis.

"And I achieved this by never backing down from a fight and always getting what I go after." James said with an arrogant pride. "That land is mine now. Lock, stock, and several legal papers with my name on them and I am not about to lose it or the dawn of my dream to a bunch of fleabags and glorified insects. Get them out of my way Danion."

"Fine." Said Danion with a slight tilt of his head. "Are your mercenaries ready?"

"They will be."

"Do they know what they're dealing with?"

"Oh yes…they definitely know what they're dealing with... and how to deal with it."

"Do they know about me?"

"No." said James.

"Good…let's keep it that way."

"Fine. What's your take on any backlash?"

"Little to none." said Danion. "Fairies are not real fighters that's why they need the Gur-Fanng. They're tough but they're not Howlers. They just want you gone. They haven't killed anyone in those logging crews though I have heard of some Gur-Fanng going to that point. Looks like this particular group won't go that far...but that could easily change with what you have planned."

"Well that's why you're here. Just in case they start acting like... Howlers."

"Oh...I see. They see the vampire, attack me first, and that gives you plenty of time to save yourself."

"Yes." James replied with no hesitation or shame.

"Well for that little statement alone I hope a large group of werewolves...whatever the pack will come rip your throat out, burn down this house, and kill you. In that order." said Danion.

"My my...why the hostility?" asked James.

"I don't like dealing with werewolves."

"I know there's bad blood but---"

"I-Don't-Like-Dealing-With-Werewolves." stressed Danion. "They bring back memories I have chosen to forget."

"I see. Well if everything goes as planned you won't have to deal with them."

"And yet I know I will not be that lucky." said Danion. "I need to go…I'm tired from the jet-lag "

"Why? We have plenty of room here." said James.

"This place is too open…and confined. I've already made other arrangements in town. Let me know how things progressed."

"Indeed I will." James said watching Danion leave through the sliding glass door to the back patio.

Danion stood there for a moment looking at the night sky then suddenly the howl of a wolf, four legged, hit his ears. His eyes seemed to be saying something. What it was I couldn't tell you but sure enough with that howl it probably had to do with Rail which was bringing a slight smile to his face…that he then quickly shrugged off.

"Focus on the task at hand." he said to himself. "There's work to be done."

And from there he took off into the air completely abandoning the feelings he once had for a werewolf to help James 'deal' with a pack of them to achieve his Camelotian dream.

Yeah…I know.

Why?

Not exactly the Danion we all know and love, right?

Sadly again…people change.

At times…not for the better.

Craig was a forest ranger…not surprising for a Gur-Fanng. It also made him a damn good spy for the OC/Gur-Fanng Alliance. He knew exactly where the logging crew was working and told the others the best time to attack. It was a simple crew of 11 men. A pre-group to get things started till the larger crew arrived. Six Gur-Fanng could easily handle them. Those who volunteer were people Craig knew and grew up with. One…Hank Marder owned the corner garage after his father. He liked to play the tough guy role but guess who was always Santa Claus at the yearly Christmas party. Another was Ann Cooper…co-owner of the Aroma Point flower shop. She and Craig dated once in high school but after their first and only date they quickly decided they were better off as friends.

Craig told the six where the 11 were and was patiently waiting for the cries of terror from yet another group of James's tree-cutters…unfortunately his werewolf ears were caught by surprise by the hail of gunfire that echoed in the distance. He immediately ran to the site and was shocked to see his friends laying at the feet of the logging crew who obviously were not loggers at all but James's mercs carrying automatic weapons loaded with silver bullets.

"Only six." the merc leader said into a cell-phone. "Piece of cake with no causalities on our side...What do you want done with the bodies?... Okay."

"So…what? We burn 'em?" a merc asked.

"Leave 'em." Said the leader.

"Leave 'em?"

"He said it will be taken care of. Now grab your gear and move out."

"What's the hurry? Isn't like we can't take care of ourselves." another merc said cocking his hand gun.

"We go in. Did the job. Get out. Get paid." said the leader. "Now move!"

The mercs were packed and off the site in less than 10 minutes. Craig then moved closer to the sight of his pack members.

His friends

Dead to the smell with their blood soaking the earth beneath them. He turned over Hank and saw the shocked look in his reverted human eyes as if he didn't believe he just been killed. Craig then went to

Ann who looked as if she was just sleeping the day away. He checked the others but it was all the same.

Dead.

Shot through the heart.

Suddenly two fairies appeared. They volunteer to wipe the memories of the loggers' minds after the Gur-Fanng were through with them. They were all ready to do the job until they saw the mercs pull out their guns and start shooting. By the time they got pass their shock it was over. The six Gur-Fanng were dead.

"What happened?" Craig asked.

"T-They just started shooting." one fairie said.

"There was nothing we could do." said the other.

"Ah…god. Oh my god." Craig said looking at the bodies.

He quickly snapped out of his own shock and got on the radio to the ranger station. Many of the other rangers were Gur-Fanng but not all so he had to keep this off the main line. He called another ranger and pack member, told them to switch to channel #3, and told him something that no Jackson Point Gur-Fanng ever wanted to hear…'The Big Bad Wolf ran into a sliver-mine.'

It was a code used through the pack of Jackson Point to signal when a Gur-Fanng had die from an unnatural death.

Mainly murdered by silver.

Word spread in no time about the six murders and the Gur-Fanng and the OC called an emergency meeting to figure out what their next move should be now that they knew that James knew what he was dealing with and knew how to 'deal' with it. The families of the murdered six wanted major pay-back for their loss…one of them being Greg Cooper, Ann's husband.

"What the hell are we standing around here for? Let's kill the sonavabitch!" he cried.

"Cooper I know how you feel---"

"My wife is dead!" Greg yelled with tears coming out of his eyes. "Don't tell me you know how I feel!"

"I lost some friends today Greg… so I do know how you feel." said Pauline Bedder, a Gur-Fanng pack leader. "But we have to tread carefully now that James knows we're werewolves…and is using silver against us."

"You think I care if he has silver?!" Greg said getting up to go after James.

"No…but you do have to worry about exposing the pack." Craig said to Greg blocking his path.

"And where the hell were you?!" Greg shouted at him. "You should've know they weren't loggers. You could've warned them…told her to stay away!"

Cooper started shoving at Craig trying to get a piece of him but a couple of Gur-Fanng held him back before things got too serious.

"Greg don't!" a Gur-Fanng named Carol said.

Her brother was one of the six that were killed with Hank and Ann. She stood between he and Craig making sure that Greg didn't get passed her.

"I want to go after James as badly as you do but not at the price of the pack." she said. "My brother would understand that...so would Ann."

Greg backed off knowing that Carol was right and started off in the other direction as Carol looked at Craig. She didn't say a word but he knew that she somewhat agreed with Greg about how Craig should have known about mercs.

Craig left the room, fell back against the wall, and slide to the floor. He sat there in the guilt of the death of his friends as Jordan came over to offer a shoulder.

"They're right…I should've known." he said.

"That's crap." said Jordan. "Think about it…James hired some triggermen who were expecting an attack… and the fact that they knew we were werewolves who could have seen that?"

"You…" Craig answered. "The other night you were worried that something like this could happen."

"Yeah..." admitted Jordan. "But I was surprised as anybody when I heard about this morning. Hey… I have lost a lot of good friends when I was living in Denver. Hell…I lost my dad and...someone else, but you know what…none of their deaths were my fault and this isn't your fault either."

"Well…it feels like it." he said.

Jordan took Craig's hand for support.

"You know whose fault this is." she told him.

"She's right buddy." Robert said to Craig in his cop uniform. "We all do."

"How did he even know?" asked Craig.

"Follow me and I'll tell you." he said leading Craig and Jordan back to the other

Gur-Fanng. "Can I have your eyes and ears on me please."

"The room all looked at Robert wondering what was up and by the look on his face it wasn't very good.

"I've just came from James's. We got a tip some teenagers were gonna try to get some pay-back for this morning. It... didn't go well." he said looking at certain Gur-Fanng in telling them their kid was involved.

"Are they dead?" a Gur-Fanng mother asked near panic.

"No." he promised them. "Bumps, bruises, and a few...broken bones."

"Broken bones!" another Gur-Fanng exclaimed.

"What is this…now he's sending hired thugs after our kids?" someone yelled.

"The kids went to attack James." Robert reminded everybody. "And it wasn't the ones from this morning that stopped them."

"Then who?" Craig asked.

"Or what?" said Jordan knowing that James couldn't stand alone against a small pack of teenage werewolves.

Robert turned and gave her a look confirming her suspicions. He took a deep breath then told the Gur-Fanng the situation.

"Our problems have just gotten a bit worse." he said.

Robert didn't show up till after most of everything happened. So I'll fill in the blanks. The five teenage Gur-Fanng, two of whom lose someone to James's mercs, decided it was time just to take him out. The self-proclaimed leader of this little pack, Roger, convinced the others with very little effort. Pain and grief has always made people open to revenge and in no time they were at James's house.

It was going to be an easy plan.

Smash in.

Rip him apart.

Leave a bloody mess.

They made their way to James's through the woods that were behind his house. In full werewolf mode they climbed up on to the back patio and were ready to strike for Gur-Fanng pride when four words stopped their approach.

"Not a good idea." Danion said sitting on a deck chair downwind from the teenagers. "Go home."

"'Sniff-Sniff'. Hey he smells... weird." another one said with a growl.

They all started picking up on Danion's scent. The House scent yet they weren't reacting the way Danion expected…charging at him in a murderous fury which meant only one thing.

"So...I'm guessing this is the first time you've seen a tone, hey kid?" Danion said to Roger.

"You're a vampire!?!"

"Bingo. Jack…tell him what he's won." Danion said in a voice that was half mocking the game show genre. "Well…he's won the knowledge that he is not the most powerful individual in the immediate area and if he leaves right now taking his friends with him he'll won't die a virgin."

Roger's yellow werewolf eyes widened at Danion's statement and in traditional teenage fashion, denied it utterly to his peers, all along panicking about how Danion knew that little fact. Vampires always know. They can smell it in the blood. You would think that werewolves could too, their hyper-sense of smell and all but no. Sure they can tell when someone just did the 'Dirty Deed', 'The Nasty', 'Knockin' Boots', 'The Wild Thing,"The---'... Sorry, it's been a while. Oh yeah…after Roger convinced everyone that he was 'not' a virgin he turned his attention back to Danion.

"You work for James." Roger growled with disgust.

"You're a smart one. So keep being smart…and go home."

"Make me." Roger said his claws ready to rip something apart.

"So now you're going for the role of mighty alpha male." Danion said with a sight rolling of his eyes. "Leading this small band of pups for the honor and the glory of the Gur-Fanng, aren't you so... unimpressive. Go home. Third and final warning."

Then Danion dismissed Roger like he wasn't worth his time. Not a good thing because everybody knows when the teenage male gets dissed action must come immediately, so with an open claw and razor sharped teeth Roger stepped up.

"In case you haven't noticed 'tone'…there's five of us and one of you." he said.

"With a raised eyebrow Danion grabbed Roger by the jacket collar and threw him into the air. When his feet came up to Danion's face he grabbed Roger by the ankles and swung him like a 'Louie-ville Slugger' against the other Gur-Fanng. One, two, three, and four, Roger's friends went flying like toys being knocked aside by a 5-year-old. Danion then flipped Roger around and set him back on his feet. His legs were buckling from the pain of being slammed against his friends and more than a few times from his head hitting the deck of the patio.

"One of you….one of me." Danion said before placing a strong upper cut that sent Roger flying several feet away from Danion's current location. "One of me…none of you."

Roger landed hard and wasn't getting up quickly but he still had enough strength to lift his head to see Danion floating over to him.

"So…you want to be leader of the pack?" he said to Roger. "Well 'pup' let me tell you what a leader should know. One…always or at least always try to know the situation you are putting your people in before committing them to it"

Danion reinforced this point by breaking Roger's left wrist. The pain of a broken bone shocked the daze out of Roger.

"Two…never underestimate anyone or anything you confront. Current case in point…you've never faced a vampire in your life but I'm sure you know about the different castes. Which one am I? Answer..." he began to say breaking Roger's other wrist. "One who is stronger than you."

Then Danion just casually broke three of Roger's fingers.

"Why did I do that? Because I could, and you needed to be reminded that if you can't handle or perform the role of leadership, you shouldn't take up its' reins."

Danion quickly saw from the corner of his eye the other Gur-Fanng teenagers gathering for an assault on him. He responded by grabbing Roger by the arm and placing his foot on the side of Roger's rib-cage.

"I can do the math…four of you and one of me. I need an equalizer. His arm is my first choice." he said to them. "Have you ever heard the sound of an arm being ripped from someone's body? It's like…a thick hotel towel being torn apart. Of course…you really don't notice because of the immense screams of pain the person is making."

The teen Gur-Fanng looked at Danion's glowing red eyes and knew that he was not making a threat but simply telling them what he was going to do.

"Don't...please." a female Gur-Fanng asked.

"Compassion...how sweet." Danion said showing very little of it himself. "But I think the only way to show you that coming out here was truly a mistake and should never be attempted again is the loss of your friend's body part."

Danion started pulling at Roger's arm. With one strong yank he could have easily ripped it off Roger's body but Danion wanted Roger to feel the pain of his skin being torn which was evident through Roger's screams. But even through Roger's cries of terror Danion's ear twitched from the familiar sound of a cocking gun.

A shot was fired.

It missed as Danion flew to the side and disappeared into the woods.

I know I said Lore don't used guns but Robert and his partner were also cops.

Do I really need to say anymore?

"Where did he go?" yelled Robert's partner.

"I don't know…just cover me while I check the kid!" said Robert.

Roger's friends crowded over him. Robert ordered them to revert back to their human form and then chastised them for being so incredibility stupid…though he used a more colorful phrase. Robert was more worried about the teens running into James's mercs, the vampire was a new surprise altogether and he never fought a vamp in his life just like most the Gur-Fanng in Jackson Point and knew that this new development was not good one.

His first priority was to get Roger and the others out of there and get Roger some medical attention but that was quickly halted by James announcing his presents.

"Thank goodness you're here officer." James said with Davies right behind him. "These band of thieves tried to break into my house. Good thing my head of security was on the job. Don't know where he is now…must have gone to try to contact the local P.D. I would like to press charges."

"Are you outta your fuckin' mind?!"

Surprising enough that didn't come from one of the teens but from Robert's partner.

"Problem officer?" James asked.

"Oh…don't bullshit us by pretending you don't know anything."

"I have no idea what you are talking about." James professed innocence.

"I believe what my partner is talking about is the incident up at your building site this morning." Robert said deciding to play James's game.

"What kind of incident?" Davis asked.

"Fatal." Robert replied.

"This morning?" James asked.

"Yes." Robert said in saying "as if you didn't know'.

"And I'm just hearing about it now?!" James shouted at Davis. "Call the lawyers, makes sure I don't have to pay the overtime for…whatever…and that those loggers are back to work first thing tomorrow."

"It was none of your crew." said Robert.

"Then who?" James said knowing the truth with a smug smile.

"You sonavabitch." Robert said angered by James's smugness.

"I beg your pardon officer?" James asked.

"Those were my friends." said Rob.

"Oh...well that changes... nothing at all." said James.

More angered Robert grabbed James by the collar showing his yellow werewolf eyes.

"Heel boy." James ordered with no fear. "Listen to me very carefully Officer... Brandon. Badge #2478931. If you're accusing me of some type of crime I'll be more than willing to head down to your station house with my lawyers of course and defend myself against your body... or 'bodies' of evidence.

There was silence to that request.

"No? Well if that's the case... "James said shrugging Robert's hands off him. "Please get off my propriety and take the 'litter' with you."

With the ego of an Roman Emperor James turned his back to them and walked away. The complete arrogance of the man was...well, do I really need to tell you? Hell…you've probably been on the receiving end of such an attitude which left you feeling helpless and most of all pissed off. So pissed off that Robert's partner went for his side-arm thinking that a couple of bullets would wipe that arrogant smile off James's face. As he aimed his gun at James it was taken out of his hands and with two gun shots Robert's partner was screaming as two bullets went into his legs. Robert turned around and instantly went into full werewolf mode to the sight of Danion holding his partner's side-arm as his partner was writhing on the ground in pain.

"Don't panic..." Danion said tossing the gun to Robert. "I think he'll recover."

Robert rushed passed Danion to check on his partner as Danion walked passed him to James.

"Taunting the police? Not real smart, but you're right, they're not going to bring charges against you. One...the un Gur-Fanng police of this town don't know a murd...unnatural death may have occrued. And two...even if there were 'bodies' of evidence presented the mystery of why they were all killed with silver bullets could and would bring the unwanted attention of certain groups. The Quinns. 109. Or worst." Danion said directing his voice to the Gur-Fanng.

"Worse?" asked Robert.

"I doubt you really want a band of Crucibles invading the small town of Jackson Point" answered Danion.

Robert shifted back into human form on that thought.

"You wouldn't." he said.

"Of course I wouldn't. I don't want the Crucibles here anymore then you do but this little...'resistance movement' you have could send a flare to any one of those three." said Danion. "And that wouldn't do any of us any good."

Again...there was silence between Danion and Robert in the meaning of 'us'.

"I can see this is a private moment between you and your people." said James.

"He's not our people!" a teen Gur-Fanng yelled insulted that James would make a similarity between a Gur-Fanng and a tone.

"Nevertheless...I'll be on my way" said James. "Have to tell the crew to start early and after this little display of things it's best I make sure the way is clear for them tomorrow. You'll be there." James spoke up with the last three words so the Gur-Fanng would hear and be wary.

Danion responded to James with a slight tilt of the head in saying 'If necessary'. James nodded himself then headed back towards the house leaving Danion alone with the Gur-Fanng.

"Tell the OC that the land now belongs to James. In my time...I've seen many people ushered off their lands by a more determined and powerful force. When they tried to fight back the results were often the same... not good. Your people are dead. Stay out of the way and no one else dies. As for the ones that are dead...mourn them, move on, and forget. In the end your life will be...somewhat better."

Danion then took into the air leaving Robert to get the teenage Gur-Fanng out of there and medical attention to his partner and Roger. Then when that was over he performed the duty of telling the rest of his pack and the OC about James and his pet vampire.

"The issue isn't whether James knew about us before or after the vampire it's that he knows about us now and knows what do to about it." Bedder said putting it on the floor.

The Gur-Fanng were at a bit of an impasse. The six deaths, the Gur-Fanng teens, and of course the appearance of a vampire. Some wanted to go on just by principle. Others kept thinking what if it was them who had been in the forest... and it frightened them. Finally someone said in a way to passing off the problem, 'Well, what do the OC say?'.

"What do you think? Jordan said in a tone that was a ridiculous question. "They've had that land for nearly 400 years. They're gonna fight to keep it."

"Well we've been the ones doing most of the fighting... and the dying. Where the hell have they been?"

"You sayin' they don't care?" asked Jordan.

"Are they here?"

"Don't be an asshole."

Who the hell are you in this?" the Gur-Fanng stated to get back for the 'asshole' comment. "You're nothing more than an outsider…not a real Gur-Fanng."

Now we all know a remark like that to 'Rail' would have landed this guy in a good trauma center but 'Jordan' was more mellow then that…and only broke his nose. With his butt hitting the floor the Gur-Fanng tried to cover his nose…and embarrassment of gushing blood. The pack looked down at him with shaking heads. This was something that was not going to be easily lived down and the two black eyes that were on their way were going to be a consent reminder of it.

"Un-good thing to say man." Craig said to his pack member.

"Really?" agreed Robert.

"Jordan's is a member of this pack." Bedder said stepping in. "She was born a Howler, yes, but she has been an adopted Gur-Fanng for over four years. She-is-one-of-us."

Bedder looked at Jordan reinsuring her on that fact. Jordan wasn't ashamed to admit it felt good to be part of a pack again after being a self-proclaimed Lone for so long.

Interesting times…which I'll tell you about them later.

"And I'm really glad about that now, since unlike most of us, Jordan actually has fought vampires."

"Brood…" the broken nose Gur-Fanng pointed out. "But what's her record with a House?"

The Gur-Fanng looked to Jordan for her answer.

"I've gone up against House before."

"And…"

"And they're not something you want to fuc--- mess with. They're smart. They're strong. They can… fly…"

Jordan paused as her mind flashed on Danion again only to quickly shrugged it off to get back to the immediate problem.

"But they can die just like Brood." she continued "Stake through the heart. Sunlight. Cutting their heads off. It's not easy but you can do it."

"What…you're saying we should take on the vampire?"

"No...I'm saying we should take him out." Jordan said as if the answer wasn't obvious. "Listen…I've taken on guys like James before too. Assholes who think they're invulnerable because of their money and power. Well ripping out their throats changed that thinking really quickly but killing James outright will just make more problems. It doesn't mean though that we still can't make him feel vulnerable by taking away the things that make him feel safe."

"The hired guns and the vampire." Craig said sensing her meaning.

"Exactly."

"If you need any help count us in." said the blond fairie Gerradenn.

She was the same one that gave John the foreman his next few weeks of nightmares about cutting down trees…and beautiful blondes. Now a lot smaller from the encounter with her wings proudly flying in the air leading a 'hover' of fairies

That's a group of fairies like a swarm of bees…if you were wondering.

"She right." Gerradenn agreed with Jordan. "James thinks this incid--- I'm so sorry...tragedy is going to keep you out of the way so he can have a clear path to our land. We can't let that happen."

"So what do you suggest…a few more Gur-Fanng for James to have target practice with?" said the broken nose Gur-Fanng.

"No." replied the fairie. "It's time for them to be the targets."

She looked at Jordan basically repeating what she said.

"There's a plan. It can work but only if the Gur-Fanng are involved. We know you have lost a lot today and we also know asking you to put you lives in danger---"

"Who said you were asking…what if you had a volunteer?" Jordan said standing out from the crowd.

"Or two." Craig said stepping up next to her.

Then there was Robert…others followed even the big-mouth broken nose Gur-Fanng.

Bedder was close to tears to see her pack standing together for the common cause of stopping James. A clear image that the Gur-Fanng was still strong even with the death of six members of their pack, it was with that Pauline realized that more death could be coming and though she probably couldn't stop it she sure could as hell keep the numbers as low as possible.

"Seems our alliance is stronger than ever." said Bedder. "We keep fighting...but with the murders this morning I don't want to take any chances, so I'm motioning that all the physical fighting be limited to those with no mates or children. Do I have a second?"

"Second it." said Craig.

What the hell are you doing?" Robert asked.

"Claire and Sara…that's what I'm doing." he answered.

Craig looked over to Jordan who was in complete agreement. Rob like a lot of others were not happy about Bedder's decision. He and a few tried to talk her out of it but Pauline stood strong and was backed-up by the single Gur-Fanngs who wanted to protect their friends. Pauline ended the discussion by leaving the room with Gerradenn to hear the fairie plan against James. Rob looked back at Craig with a look that could strangle. Craig looked back with an expression saying, "Be as pissed off as you want I'm glad I did it.'

"Great. Just great.' said Rob. "Stuck on the sidelines."

"I think your wife and daughter will have no problem with that." said Craig.

Rob gave a growl of frustrating anger.

"Rob…I wasn't much older than Sara when I lost my dad and trust me…I really wished he was around when I was growing up so let's not take that away from your daughter if we can help it."

Part of him wanted to disagree but the other part just couldn't

"Ahh…helpless." he said over the situation.

"Ahh…come on buddy." Craig said. "Besides I know you can't wait to wear that uniform and gear for the first boy who comes a callin' for Sara's first date."

The three had a small laugh over that when something came to Jordan looking at Rob's uniform.

"Rob...maybe you can be more help than you think." she said.

As Jordan explained Pauline finished hearing the OC's plan for James.

"Sounds risky." Bedder said concerned about her people.

"But we'll still win." said Gerradenn.

"Yeah Gerri but for how long? I may have been all brave and self-assured in there, but I can also see a lot more dead Gur-Fanng, and us still not stopping James."

"Don't say that."

"I think it needs to be said." Bedder pointed out. "Six dead bodies and we didn't have a clue that James knew."

"The Elders wanted me to express their deepest regrets over your lost. Your people were protecting our land for us and they were killed because of it." Gerradenn said putting her tiny hand on Bedder's shoulder. "I know there are no words I can say that can make you feel better…but we are sorry and we're not going to let this 'Novack' get away with it."

"I know that…and thank-you but your plan is a short-term solution at best." said Bedder. "James has the advantages here. Y'know it always amazes me how little and yet how much power the humans have and the majority don't even know it."

That's a good thing for Lore…trust me.

"James has the money, the weapons, and worse of all doesn't have to worry about the Quinns or 109." Said Bedder.

"That's probably why he left your people out in the open…to scare you into backing off, to show you that he could expose you. He knew that you were not about to let the police find those bodies and start asking the wrong questions. Bastard. Well don't worry…next time we'll be leaving the bodies,"

Suddenly an idea sparked in Pauline's mind. One if it worked right would be a definite surprise for James. All it took was a sight modification to the OC's plan. She told Gerradenn and the fairie agreed that it just might work.

"All right…I'll go tell the others."

"And I'll tell the OC and the Elders."

"Cross your wing Gerri." said Bedder.

"Gerradenn watched as Pauline left hoping her friend's plan to stop James really would work. Then she remembered she had to get back to the other OC to let them in on the new plan. She started on her way when out of nowhere a raven-haired fairie appeared in her path.

"So…the Gur-Fanng had no idea about James knowing they were werewolves." said Lee-Shannon. "Even after we told you and the Elders he did…and hired mercenaries who knew as well."

There was a clear hint of fear in Gerradenn's eyes as she stared at the black clothed fairie…of course members of the Consortia tend to do that.

"How long have you been here?" asked Gerradenn.

"Long enough to know that you've been keeping information---important information from your allies. Why...afraid if they knew James's hired guns had silver they wouldn't fight anymore?" said Lee-Shannon. "Of course now they're truly motivated to fight for the OC cause. Well...more manipulated."

"It's not like that."

"Really...why don't we let them decide that?" Lee-Shannon said starting to move in the direction of the Gur-Fanng.

"No." Gerradenn said hovering in her way."

"Scared? You should be. Do you have any idea what would happen to the OC/Gur-Fanng alliance if this ever go out? Not just in Jackson Point but everywhere."

Gerradenn avoided eye contact from Lee-Shannon not doing a good job in hiding her shame. Then Gerradenn voiced an opinion that explained the OC's action...or justified them.

"Well maybe if the Consortia lend a hand---"

"The Consortia is not here to protect you from James---"

"No...it's here to tell us to give up our land to him."

"I know how important the land is to the OC especially to the fairies but not as important as not exposing the Lore or loss of life. Apparently…you and the Elders don't think the same. Six-Dead-Gur-Fanng'

"Are you going to tell them?" Gerradenn asked frightful of what the answer.

Lee-Shannon stared at her in silence secretly wanting Gerradenn to sweat before she gave an answer.

"No…" said Lee-Shannon. "For now."

"Other than the Consortia, the OC, and the Gur-Fanng show that different Lore can work together…even in a fruitless cause but the Consortia hasn't gotten the best reputation like you and Gur-Fanng. I honestly don't want to see the two groups separate and make other Lore believe that the only way to avoid betrayal is to stick among their own. That is something that definitely would not help the Lore." said Lee-Shannon. "Of course…this does give me the bargaining chip to convince you and the Elders to give up your little crusade and move on."

"No…there's a plan."

"Doom to failure I'm sure."

You don't know that, let us try." Gerradenn asked with a plea in her voice. "Come on…you were OC before you became Consortia."

Gerradenn knew it was beneath her but she was also desperate and compared to the alternative of losing faire land she could live with it.

"Very well 'sister'. Let's see if your plan works." said Lee-Shannon. "But make no mistake if it doesn't I'm expecting this tribe of fairies to move on to protect the rest of us. Refusal could mean certain information gets to the Gur-Fanng. I may not want to destroy the OC/ Gur-Fanng alliance but it doesn't mean I won't."

With that unsettling threat Lee-Shannon flew off leaving Gerradenn to ponder her morals over the situation. Not only was she apart of deceiving the Gur-Fanng but also her friend of many years Pauline Bedder. She truly hoped that her plan to keep James away from OC land worked because if it didn't…everyone was basically screwed.

The sun hadn't yet started it's morning shift over Jackson Point or the neighboring forest. James's mercs who were at the logging site waited for the early crew to arrive. Their job…making sure that the werewolves didn't decide to make another run at stopping James's construction plans. The 11 men hid in the woods not worried about any confrontation that might come but more that it might not come at all. The tools they had to end any conflict quickly filled those men with an abundance of confidence...however the 12th member of their group didn't share in that confidence.

"Scared?" the merc leader known as 'the Major' asked Danion.

"Just a little concerned that's all." he answered.

"I doubt anything will happen. How stupid do you have to be to come back to a place where you know you're gonna die?"

"About as stupid as waiting to take on super-natural creatures in hope of getting into a fight" replied Danion. "No doubt about it Major, you and your men got the hardware that gives you a distinct advantage...but I've taken on a few werewolves now and then and I venture to say I know better than to confront them in their natural habitat."

"We seemed to do alright yesterday."

Yesterday you caught them by surprise. Today...they'll know better and much to the disbelief of you and Mr. James werewolves are pretty intelligent. Of course, pissing them off makes them completely unreasonable." Danion said remembering Rail with a slight smile. "Now I know I'm no 'Military' leader like yourself but I would think the killing of six of my pack would not make me all that reasonable.... do you?"

"If that's the case why are you here?"

"Because like you I have a job that needs to be done but don't worry I'll be long gone by the time dawn shines its bright little head..."

"What?"

"Shhh! Listen." said Danion.

The Major listened and heard nothing for the first few seconds then caught the sounds of moving brush in the distance. He gave a bird whistle sign to his men as he looked at Danion, impressed by his sharp ear.

The mercs took covering positions and waited as the sounds of movement came closer to them until two Gur-Fanng in human form came into sight. One of the mercs took aim but the Major stopped him wanting to make sure the two were really werewolves and not hikers passing by. Danion took one look and knew telling the Major to shoot. The two quickly ducked the bullets that were coming for them, saw the mercs, went into full werewolf mode, and took off into the forest.

"How could you have missed?!" the Major yelled at his man.

"Because they heard the cocking of your guns. I'm surprised the whole forest didn't hear it." said Danion not surprised by what happened.

"Pursue." the Major ordered.

"Following them deeper into the forest would not be a good idea---"

"If you're scared leave now." an annoyed Major said wondering why Danion was even there. "Move out. Standard pattern. Night-scopes."

The mercs followed the Major's orders and headed out to hunt Gur-fang.

"Leave...and miss all the carnage?" Danion said to himself in a sarcastic tone. "Now why would I want to do that?"

He followed the mercs who were combing the area in a straight line with about by 10 to 12 feet between each man. They slowly walked forward always keeping one eye one their surrounding and another on each other…a task made easy with their night-vision goggles.

That was their first mistake.

Night-goggles amplify light so you can see in the dark so what happens when a really bright light shines in front of you? A fairies' light burst can already easily blind someone (remember Zarafinn and Clipboard). Now imagine seeing that same light amplified 100 times.

Ever look at the sun through binoculars.

The light came from the end of the merc line hitting the last merc directly in the face and temporary blinding the other in front of him. The last merc's cries of pain alerted the others and when they turned back around the last merc was gone…disappeared from sight. The 'second to last' didn't even have a change to say anything before a very sharp arrow was sticking out of his throat killing him.

"What the hell is going on?" The Major said.

Distracted by what they just saw two other mercs suddenly felt the pain of arrows entering their legs, but before them could fully react to the pain they were rushed tackled and dragged into the cover of the forest darkness. The Major quickly ordered his men to come together back to back so all sides were covered. There was a dead silence in the area with triggers ready to pull and with a snap of a twig the night was filled with gunfire.

Just before that Danion was entering the area where the mercs were when he tripped over something. He looked down and found the missing mercs…their bodies buried up to his face with mouth and nostrils filled with dirt.

"Uh oh." he said knowing what that meant.

He then saw the merc with the arrow through his throat. At first…he thought the arrow was a sign that the Gur-Fanng were ready for him but he blew a quick sigh of relief seeing that the arrow metal-tipped and useless against him…still the meaning behind the arrow wasn't a good one. When Danion heard the gunfire echoing through the forest he quickly moved to its source and saw the Major and his men standing over the bodies of several Gur-Fanng.

"What happened?" he asked.

"You were right…they tried to ambush us but we got them all."

Danion looked down at the Gur-Fanng in their human form and slightly tilted his head.

"Nooo...not really." he said.

"What?"

"They're-still-alive!" Danion shouted.

Suddenly a Gur-Fanng rose up and grabbed a merc's gun shooting him with it. The others followed going into full werewolf mode and attacking the mercs. More surprises came as two of the mercs were pulled underground by their ankles and arrows hit the mark of another. If it wasn't for Danion's quick vampire reflexes the Major himself would have had an arrow in the center of his forehead.

"Get your men out of here!" yelled Danion.

But it was too late…each of the surviving mercs were surrounded by the Gur-Fanng. Danion looked at the situation and slowly noticed that the Gur-Fanng were not killing the mercs in the traditional style of ripping them apart unfortunately this slight distraction made him wide open for attack by charging Gur-Fanng. Now a House is definitely stronger than one Gur-Fanng or two, probably even three but five or seven?

Hey…the kid's a vampire not Superman.

Don't worry someone as seasoned as Danion learned long ago to overcome the strength of superior numbers. In this case using a large branch to smack the Gur-Fanng…of course I'm sure his ability to fly over them helped. However, over-powering Danion was only the first part of the plan…moving him into position was the other. Here's something you can use if you ever get into this situation. When you can't fly and you're fighting someone who can they rarely expect one thing... being attacked from above. Something Danion immediately discovered as a werewolf drove out of a tree and sank 'her' fangs into his shoulder. The pain was excruciating making Danion loose concentration and fall from the sky. The two crashed at the top of a steep hill and went tumbling down that hill with the werewolf's teeth still in Danion shoulders. When they reached the bottom he quickly got up and recovered in time to stop a wooden knife from going into his heart. Danion knocked the knife out of her claws then

simply just reached behind himself to the back of the werewolf's jacket collar to throw her off him.

"Clever bringing in the gnomes to attack from underground. And the elves…not only the best archers but part of the OC." Said Danion. "It won't work though…kill these men and James will just have another squad here in 48 hours. And that---"

She didn't give him time to finish his sentence as she charged at Danion. He tried to move aside but wasn't fast enough as she caught him by the arm with her fangs. Pain again went rushing through Danion but he rode it out better this time.

"Let go of me." he said once then twice while keeping her from clawing at his face.

Frustrated and quite honestly just pissed off he popped out his own fangs and sank them into Jordan's neck.

What…you thought it was going to be someone else?

The pain from Danion's bite made her reel back and let go of his arm freeing him to grab Jordan by the jacket and shirt collar and pinning her against a tree.

"Not a fun time when someone sinks their fangs into your flesh is it?" he said spitting out little hairs from his teeth then noticing the extra garment under her shirt. "Bulletproof vest. Haven't seen that trick in…a long time."

Still feeling the pain Jordan was about to make a wisecrack when she looked down and got a look at 'her vampire'.

A very good look.

"Oh…my god." she said reverting back to human form and showing a stunned face. "Danion?"

Surprised obviously that she knew his name he took a closer look at her. It took a few seconds but he recognized the face. Jordan seeing him brought the beginnings of a smile to her face…only to have it cut short by Danion letting go of her collar and putting a firm grip around her throat.

"She's…Dead. I don't know how you found out about her but you have made one serious mistake in using this fairie trick!" he exclaimed with a voice of intensified anger as he slammed the back of her head against the tree…more than once. "You didn't even have the gray-matter or respect to look exactly like her."

He tightened his grip on her blocking the air to her lungs causing her to get lightheaded.

"At one time…I thought James's idea to stop you was a bit extreme but now those thoughts are gone!"

His eyes filled with glowing red rage Danion kept squeezing at Jordan's throat. He probably would have killed her if it wasn't for the small miracle of day-break. He noticed the surrounding darkness getting brighter and made the quick decision of throwing Jordan aside…hard…to take shelter.

"Listen to me very carefully you little flea--- Little girl. Do not ever think about using her against me ever again…and as for this little war you are having... it's-over! You…the OC…and the rest of the

'Green-Fang' will turn this land over to James" he ordered turning to leave "...Or be wiped out."

Danion then took off into the air not going above the trees knowing the thick brush of the forest would block the sunlight till he could get to safety. Seeing him taking off Jordan tried to yell out to him but couldn't get enough air through her choked throat to barely manage a whisper.

"Danion... Danion!" she yelled in a horsed voice that couldn't be heard. "It's me...It's me."

She couldn't chase after him with her head still hurting from being slammed against the tree. Also…losing oxygen may make you black out but so can the sudden rush of it going back to your head. Jordan could feel what was coming and couldn't do anything to stop it.

"Damn it..." she said as her eyes fell shut into unconsciousness.

And with that our two lovers were reunited…though admittedly not the most romantic of reunions. Now I know what you're thinking…this doesn't bode well for things to come.

You don't know the half of it.

2

When Jordan woke up and found herself home in her own bed she stayed there for an hour wondering if what she saw was real or fantasy.

No!

It was him.

It was Danion.

The next hour was determining how this was possible and the hour after that was a swear-fest of how stupid she was to let that 'bitch' Phil-el trick her that fucking vampire dust. The last couple of hours were filled with anger, tears, and happiness. Anger at herself for being so easily duped. Tears over all the time that was wasted that she could have looked for Danion…maybe even found him and them being together and happiness that now they could be together... as soon as she could find and convince him that she wasn't a fairie illusion.

She then heard a knocking at the apartment's front door and Kefflynn's voice as she let Craig and Claire inside the apartment to see how their friend was doing after her encounter with the vampire.

"She's been in her room all day." said Keff.

"So…she's awake?" Craig asked.

"Has been for hours." Keff said. "But she's wants to be alone for a while."

"What was she thinking jumping on that vamp's back?" said Craig.

"That I could get the drop on him and dust him before he knew what happened." Jordan answered coming out of her bedroom. "It…didn't work."

"You alright, J?" asked Claire.

"Yeah." Jordan said showing no worries.

"How's the throat?" Keff asked her.

"Not a mark on me." she said showing a clean neck that just hours before had five deep impressions from Danion's fingers.

That werewolf hyper-healing.

"We were really worried about you." said Claire. "After they found you knocked out and no word all day---"

"All day?" asked Jordan.

"Yeah…it's almost Three in the afternoon." Keff said pulling the shades to let in the sun.

"Whoa! Close the shades!" Jordan said blocking her eyes. "The sun gotten brighter all of a sudden?"

"That's what happens when you spent all day in a darken room." Keff said closing the shades.

"Here…Sara made this for you." Claire said handing Jordan a colored piece of construction paper.

It was fold in half with a happy face design, rainbows, and stars. When she opened it up there were three big multi-colored words splashed across inside,

'GET BETTER SOON.'

"Ohh…that's so sweet." Jordan smiled. "Thank her for me--- You told her?"

"No…she thinks you fell on a hike." said Claire.

"This should also put a smile on your face...Bedder's plan worked."

"Yes!"

"All construction has stopped till the investigation is over." said Claire.

"Which will probably be a very long time." said Craig.

"Robby was there for the whole thing…said James was not happy. Vampire was there too." said Claire.

"What did they do...I mean, uh...nothing stupid." Jordan said trying not to reveal anything.

"They didn't see him but they knew he was there." Claire said touching the end of her nose. "Doesn't really matter now…we've won!"

"Don't be too sure about that…James probably has a back-up plan." said Craig. "So we better be ready for it… I don't plan on being caught off guard again."

Suddenly Claire kissed Craig on the cheek.

"What's that for?" he asked.

"For seconding Bedder's order to keep mates and family out of the fighting." she said. "Keeps me from worrying about my hubby. Now…the only thing I have to worry about is you two…of course there's an easy way to fix that..."

She boldly showed off her wedding ring twisting it around her finger to Jordan and Craig clearly expressing the meaning behind her statement which wasn't getting lost on Jordan.

"Go home." she said to Claire.

"But---"

"Go home."

"Alright…but we'll talk about this later." Claire said heading for the door. "Think about it."

Claire then left leaving Jordan and Craig in an awkward situation again.

"You have to admire her persistence." said Craig."

"Or strangle her for it." said Jordan.

"Can I... uh, speak to you alone for a minute... outside." asked Craig.

"Sure." Jordan said slightly confused by the request.

She looked over to Kefflynn who gave Jordan the 'Go-Go' sign with her hands to talk to Craig outside in the hall.

"Listen…when I saw you on the ground last night not moving…the things that went through my mind…"

"Sorry that I scared you." she said.

"Well…the thing that really scared me was... Look…I really care about you."

"Craig..."

"I know you don't feel the same way I've accepted that…and pretty soon I'll actually mean it." he confessed then continued. "I don't want you to fight anymore."

"What?"

"I don't want you to fight anymore."

The statement sparked a memory back in Denver. The Decennial, Danion saying the same thing, her wanting him to say it, and both knowing full well that she was going to fight anyway. The feelings it brought back made Jordan instantly caress her bracelet tattoo all the while not hearing Craig's words until the very end.

"... I just don't want to worry about you…okay?" he finished.

"First of all..." she said back-kicking her apartment door to keep nosy fairies from overhearing. "You don't have to worry about me. I've taken care of myself for a long time."

"Well you're not by 'yourself' anymore." Craig pointed out. "And there's nothing wrong with someone worrying about you it just means someone cares."

A small laugh came out of Jordan.

"You're laughing at me." he said.

"No." she promised. "It's just that my grandmother said the same thing one time."

"Really…where's she now?"

"Denver…we haven't talked in a while." she said.

"Why?"

"A long story I really don't want to get into right now."

"Okay…I'll go now but think about what I said."

"Between you and Claire I'll be thinking a lot tonight." she said.

As Craig left Jordan went back into her apartment seeing Kefflynn rubbing the side of her face.

"Hope I didn't knock anything loose." said Jordan.

"Not much." Keff answered. "Craig's a nice guy."

"Yes he is."

"But he can't match up to Danion…can he?"

"What?" Jordan said, with widen eyes and a turned head.

"Danion. That's was his name…right?"

"H-How?"

"I checked up on you while you sleeping and you mumbled a name... 'Danion...don't go'"

Jordan lowered her head and closed her eyes. Even with the excuse of blacking out she still shook her head of how stupid she was to let something like that slip.

"I know you don't want to talk about it and I'm gonna sound like a complete and total bitch but it's time to give up the ghost." Keff said. "He's dead… you're alive. It's time to start living---"

"He's not dead." said Jordan.

"What?"

"He-not-dead." she repeated very clearly. "I thought he was…all this time I thought he was but he' wasn't. I saw him...last night...he was there."

"Last night?" asked Keff hovering closer to Jordan. "What…he was one of the mercenaries?"

Jordan was hesitant to answer.

"No..."

"Then who…an elf? 'Cause the only other one out there was the vamp and I know you wouldn't---"

Kefflynn looked at Jordan's face and saw the silence of her eyes speaking volumes.

"Titania's eye" Keff said in disbelief. "You...and a vampire?"

Immediately Jordan grabbed Keff out of the air to make one point clear to her.

"No-One-Knows." ordered Keff. "No one."

"Okay…no one knows." she said seeing seriousness in Jordan's eyes.

She let Keff go and there was a quietness between them but Jordan knew it was going to break with one question.

"How---?"

"Denver." Jordan answered her question before she asked it. "We met when I was still living in Denver. He uh…saved my life."

And so again the story of Danion and Rail was told. This time with the added characters of Price, Phil-el, Granny P and what the three did to break our loving couple up which finished with their reunion the night before.

"Then I passed out." Jordan said with frustration. "For 12 years I thought he was dead…and he wasn't. 12... fucking years I've been mourning him. 12 fucking years I could've been looking. 12---"

"---Fucking years probably wasting your time. House Vampires have a big rep of knowing how to and staying gone." said Keff. "You would have never have found him."

"Well I'm gonna find him now." she said.

"And let him finish the job he started last night?!"

"He didn't believe it was me last night he thought it was a fairie trick. 'I can't blame him if someone tried to use Danion against me I be so pissed off...''

Suddenly something sparked in her mind. A revelation about Danion.

"He was pissed. He wanted to kill me." she said thinking about it.

"Exactly…which is why you should stay away---"

"No…you don't understand." explained Jordan." He thinks I'm dead...but he hasn't forgotten me. He still remembers me. He still loves me. Keff you gotta help me find him."

"How?"

"Hit the OC Grapevine." she asked. "No matter how good a House is in covering their tracks it can't be that hard to find one in a town full of werewolves."

"Well he's probably staying at James."

"No…he'll probably wanna stay somewhere safe during the day and that's not James's."

"Still…this may not be a good idea, J. Looks like your boyfriend has gone 'Vader' since Denver. Helping you with the Quinns to helping James steal our land…why?"

Jordan couldn't deny her confusion over that fact. Why would Danion be working for James? She thought back to who Danion was 12 years ago and knew the idea would be laughable. She also thought back to who she was 12 years ago and sadly had to admit she wouldn't have given a 'rat's ass' about fairies losing their land to James but that was a long time ago and a lot of things had happened to change Rail to Jordan. So…it was only natural to assume that a lot of things had happened to change Danion.

But what?

"I don't know." said Jordan. "I'll just have to ask him when you find him."

Rolling back the clock to 10:23 in the AM on the same day, James's breakfast was ruined by the bad news from Danion.

"All of them?" James asked.

"I don't know what happened to the Major but as for the rest...dead and gone."

"What happened?"

"You underestimated the opposition to your construction plan." said Danion. "They fought back and won...for now that is."

"So…what now?"

"Now...you open the front door."

The doorbell rang and James raised an eyebrow to Danion's 'E.S.P.' which was simple enhanced hearing James snapped his fingers to Davis to greet whoever was at the door. Davis went and returned saying the police and someone from the D.A.'s office wanting to speak to James. As James turned around to asked Danion what he thought this was about and he was taken back by Danion's sudden disappearance.

"Show them in." James said so his guest could hear.

Two police officers came into the room, Rob and his partner. The person with them was a young A.D.A. who was human and about to give James more bad news with his breakfast.

"Murders? Who?" James asked pretending complete ignorance.

"That's what we're hoping you know, sir." said the A.D.A. "They were on your property and word has it there's been some trouble out there."

"Environmentalist. Nothing I can't deal with." said James looking at Rob and remembering him from before.

"Well…if you could take a look at these pictures---"

"There's no need for me to look at those pictures." said James. "Since I don't know what happened up there I doubt I'll know anyone involved."

"Please sir…take a look." the A.D.A. insisted.

The truth was James didn't know the mercs. His only contact was with the Major. They both preferred it that way. He looked at the photos of the mercs broken bodies shaking his head at the knowledge of knowing them.

"Bloody." said James.

"Some were shot…others had their necks broken. A couple had some unidentified wounds…while another pair seemed to be partially buried."

"Buried?" asked James. "That's weird."

"About as weird as the ones that were shot…the bullets were removed from their bodies."

"Removed? Oh...to keep them from being matched to a weapon." said James.

"That would be our guess. Obviously they were soldiers…maybe mercenaries. Why they were out there we don't know. Maybe a weapons deals gone bad or some kind of double-cross. Right now it's a mystery until our investigation is over."

"Well…I'll help in any way I can." said James.

"Good…then you'll understand why we'll asked you to stop all construction in that area till further noticed."

"I beg your pardon?" James asked.

"We have a crime scene up in those hills Mr. James." said the A.D.A. 'Bodies with no I.D.s and probably will never be I.D.ed. Our best bet for some answers is the area where they died. Perhaps a stray bullet in a tree…a foot print somewhere…a dropped gun on or off a trail. We won't know till we start searching but if your construction continues you could inadvertently destroy evidence. We understand this is a major inconvi---"

"Inconvenience? Do you know how much money I'll lose when the construction doesn't go through on time?"

"5428 dollars a---"

"Shut-up Davis!" James yelled. "I can't accept this. This is not happening."

"I'm sorry sir, but it is happening."

"No, you don't understand. This-is-not-happening." repeated James.

His tone was obviously meant as an order and the A.D.A. knew it. So in response he had an 'order' himself…in paper form.

"Yes…it is." the A.D.A said pulling a document out of his briefcase. "And this court order confirms it."

"A court order can easily be changed." said James.

"Yes it can…but until such time if your logging crews show up to work that land they will be arrested…as will you for breaking the law." said the A.D.A. "And let me tell you...the judge who signed that

"Trolls?"

"They're a distance cousin of the OC but never fully accepted into the whole. It's cause some…bad blood between them on more than one occasion." said Danion. "They'll do the job for you…if properly motivated."

"Motivated in…?" James asked but knew by rubbing his fingers together.

"Gold. Gold coins if you have them but gold of any kind will make a troll your lap-dog and since they already hate the OC there shouldn't be any problems."

"So…where do you get them?"

"I've already found some earlier this morning." said Danion. "All I need is the gold to secure their services"

Again an eyebrow raised on James to Danion's new determination on the situation that wasn't there before.

"A few days ago you were telling me to move my building because of minor problems. Now you're telling me to hire troll hitmen. Why the sudden turn around?" he asked.

"Let's just say I've become very…motivated against the OC and leave it at that." said Danion with a dead stare. "The gold?"

"I can get it." said James.

"By tomorrow."

"Tomorrow?" said Davis.

"How much by tomorrow?" asked James.

"More than little. More than a lot." answered Danion.

"And you expect me to get that by tomorrow?" said James.

"If you want the OC off your land…yes." said Danion.

"Even if your plan does work there still this to deal with…" James said holding up the court order.

"That's your department not mine." said Danion. "I'll call you later to give more details about the gold…then we-will-end-this."

"Later? It's daylight…where are you going?"

"I have to get back to the trolls and tell them the deal's on. The brush of the trees will protect me." he said.

Danion headed to the back door and hesitated at the long distance of 70 feet to the tree line.

"You'll get that land." Danion said to James.

He pulled his coat over his head and ran to the tree line. He was a little singed and smoky but nothing that wouldn't heal in an hour. He made his way through the forest on foot, he could have flown but was worried about a stray ray of sunlight hitting him and walking made it easier to avoid the light…except for the one that was heading straight for him.

"What do you want?" Danion asked.

"I heard what happened last night." said Lee-Shannon

"Yeah…the great OC/Gur-Fanng uprising."

"With a court order to boot."

"You knew about that?"

"Just found out. I knew that last night the Gur-Fanng were planning something but it being legal...?" said Lee-Shannon.

They were both surprised that Lore would use human laws to protect themselves but hey… it worked didn't it.

"Last night? You knew they were up to something last night and you didn't tell me?" said Danion.

"I didn't know what the whole the plan was exactly and even if I did I couldn't have told you." said Lee-Shannon. "If you would have known what their plan was and prepared for it the OC and Gur-Fanng would have started to realized that someone inside or close to the inside was working against them…and I would probably be high on the list of candidates since I'm already been telling to OC to let James have the land. Now I'm sure you'll understand how bad this would of made things for the Consortia."

"Oh…what a shame that would be." said Danion not really meaning it. "I have been forced to be with James for nearly two years for the Consortia… when do I get my life back?"

"It was my understanding that you did get your life back 7 years ago... then you had a repeat of the '91 incident 4 years later. So now you are here fulfilling your task, but at least this time you don't have to do three just one and that's it." directed Lee-Shannon.

"Ah, yes...working undercover for the Consortia as a henchman for a megalomanic." said Danion. "Of course I could probably do the job a whole lot better if I had good intel beforehand."

"Like I said I didn't know the whole plan and I only found out about the court order this morning."

"Was that before or after your little sex-romp?"

"W-What?"

"Sex." Danion said. "I'm sure it's a concept you're familiar with since you've just recently had it and apparently...'sniff' with more than one individual."

"How did you know---"

"I can smell it on you...please bathe afterwards."

"I knew vamps had heightened senses but..."

"And since you've obviously been in close 'contact' with other fairies... what have you told them about me?"

"Nothing."

"Well you must have said something cause last night I was confronted by..."

Danion quickly shut up. The anger from what he still thought was a faire trick was revealing things that he didn't want revealed.

"What?" Lee-Shannon asked.

"Nothing." he lied. "I was just confronted by a ghost."

"What kind of ghost?"

"One that was quite upsetting and frankly none of your business." Danion made clear to her. "In the end…it was nothing more than a cruel illusion."

"Whatever you saw last night I had nothing to do with it. The OC's not supposed to know that we're working together remember? Besides I don't know anything about you myself other than the general file that Walsh gave me…and those never have the full story." She exclaimed.

Danion let his anger subside to logic. Lee-Shannon couldn't have known about Rail. The only people who did weren't around to tell the OC so who the hell was that last night? He had a faint thought he knew couldn't be possible. A thought oddly enough he didn't want to be possible.

Could it have really been Rail?

No…but if that was true how did that Gur-Fanng know his name?

Danion pushed it out of his mind and focused back to the OC by telling Lee-Shannon about his plans with the trolls…she wasn't really pleased about it.

"You're going to kill fairies?" she said with a stunned looked.

"Not a lot…I hope."

"That wasn't part of the plan."

"I have changed the plan for expeditiousness. If the Elders need motivation I will give them motivation. Then when they do what the Consortia wants them to do my job is done and I will leave this place never to return again." said Danion moving pass Lee-Shannon to get back to the trolls.

The look in his eyes worried her. There was a plan and killing her own kind was not a part of it…how ironic since she threatened her own earlier. She immediately took out an ultra-mini cellphone from her coat and started punching in numbers."

"It's me... What's wrong? I got a psychopathic vampire on my hands... Trolls…he wants to use trolls against the OC....What?!, Well I hope you do 'cause we've worked too hard to see things go to shit now... Fine." she said then shutting closed the cell while shaking her head over recent developments. "This better be all worth it in the end."

Fast-forwarding the clock to 10:13 in the PM at the Murdock Hotel. Danion walked into the hallway of the third floor from the roof entrance, He was ready for a good night sleep that he usually took during the day, but his deal with the trolls took all day. They wanted it all up front and Danion was adamant in only giving them half before the job and the rest when it was over. The trolls complained because frankly they were greedy. Danion explained he could always take his business and gold somewhere else. This seemed to close the deal very quickly. He turned the key of the door when he heard charging footsteps heading for him. He turned and barely caught a broom handle from hitting his face but the broom was only a distraction to get a clear foot-shot at Danion's sternum which knocked him backwards into his room.

"That's for slamming me against the tree." Jordan said coming into the room and closing the door behind her.

She then took a frame-glass picture off the wall and shattered it over Danion's head.

"That's for nearly choking me to death." she said not finished quite yet.

For that she firmly landed a foot squarely between his legs.

"And that's for working with James you son of a bitch!" she cried looking at Danion on the floor as he curled himself up as we all males do when we're hit that way.

You would think this would not be a happy moment for Danion but he rolled over and looked up at her with an expression saying 'There's no denying it now'.

"It is you." he said.

She came down and laid on top of him breathing heavily as she got nose to nose with Danion.

"Damn right it's me." she said.

With no hesitation Jordan kissed Danion on the lips with a passion of someone who…quite frankly thought her lover was dead for 12 years, and was determined to make up for last time.

"How?" he asked breaking off the kiss.

"Later?" she said continuing the kiss.

"Now."

Aww, fine...shit." she said frustrated that Danion rather talk than celebrate that they were both alive and together again.

Can you blame her?

But the sooner she could explain things the sooner they could 'celebrate', so Jordan told Danion everything about the plan that was hatched up by his so-called friend Price and her Granny P. and how she was tricked by that 'bitch' Phil-el.

"... And I just left after that. I yelled at my grandmother for what she did and just left." she finished. "God...I was such a fuckin' idiot."

"You weren't the only one." he said. "I really need to visit my old 'friend' Price when this is over."

"Ohh...definitely."

"And you should go see your grandmother."

"Why?"

"To make up." he said.

"I haven't seen her in 12 years. I have no need to see her."

"You hate her because you think I killed myself because she tricked me into thinking you killed yourself. Now that you know I'm alive you can give up your hate and have a relationship with her again."

"Well you're forgiving."

"Oh...trust me I will not be the same way when I see Price and Phil-el again."

"So when do we leave?"

"There is no 'We'. You will go see your grandmother."

"I…send her a postcard every now and then." said Jordan. "Have been for the last six years."

Danion looked at her with a lot of surprise after her last statement about Granny P.

"You're right…she still my grandmother but I still haven't forgiven her for what she did."

"Your grandmother did a bad thing for a good reason. Of course she went overboard listening to Phil-el."

"They were afraid you'd change your mind and come running back to me." said Jordan walking up behind Danion and slipping her hand into his. "Would you have?"

"No." he said taking his hand away from Jordan's. "Your Granny P. made some good points to me that's why I left."

Immediately Jordan tried to throw a left cross into Danion's jaw but he grabbed her fist before she could make contact.

"I'm still mad about that." she said with the mixed expression of anger and hurt.

"Understandable."

"'I'm sorry?!...I'm sorry?!' Two lousy words on a piece of paper?" she said recalling the memory. "I deserved better than that."

"Yes...you did." Danion agreed. "And that's my fault but I thought... just leaving quick and easy would better."

"For me or for you?"

Danion acknowledged that scenario with a tilt of his head.

"What could I have said?" asked Danion. "'Yes...I care about you. Yes...I want to be with you but your grandmother was right. In the end it wouldn't have worked...and I was just too caught up in the moment to see that. I didn't see the long-term effects on you or me...mostly you."

"So you left because you cared about me?" she said in a slightly sarcastic tone but secretly hoping that was the answer.

"I left because it was the right thing to do."

"And because you still loved me?"

Her dramatic change from 'care' to 'love' brought silence to Jordan's inquiry from Danion. He wanted to say it. It was the truth but he went for changing the subject."

"I'm glad you're not dead." he told her.

"Well I'm happy about that, too…and that you're not dead either." she told him.

Danion slightly tilted his head again to that statement.

"What?" Jordan asked.

"Nothing."

"What?" she repeated for an answer.

He thought about it for a moment and then just told her.

"When your grandmother told me that you killed yourself and the reason why I felt so guilty for what I did I decided to kill myself." he said. "Ironically enough if it wasn't for Price I be dead now."

Jordan's mind flashbacked to 12 years ago at the Cliffton Hotel when she was crying over a pile of dust that wasn't Danion. She remembered how she was convinced by 'that bitch' it was Danion, saying things like he was crying and wondering if they would go to the same place. Knowing this information was true was a good way for Phil-el to sell Danion's death. Jordan also realized it was the best way that Phil-el could bring more pain to her over Danion's death.

This revelation however didn't upset Jordan as much as knowing that Danion was going to kill himself because he thought he was caused her death and wanted to be with her in…whatever place. It was the stuff that made writer's famous(hint-hint) but to Jordan it was a reminder of why Danion was the 'One'. She moved towards him wanting to hold him, kiss him, and just be near him…only to be stopped by him.

"Don't." he said.

"Why?"

"Rail…"

"Jordan." she corrected.

"What?"

"Jordan. I dropped Rail a long time ago."

The tip of Danion's mouth slightly curved into a smile on this information.

"What?" she asked again.

"Jordan?"

"Yeah?" confused by the humor of it.

"That's your name? The name you said you would kick my ass if I ever called you by it? The name you swore you only tell me after you were dead, buried, and a ghost…so I still wouldn't hear it?" he said. "Jordan. That's the big secret?"

"It's my middle name."

"And... what's the first?"

"Do I look dead to you?" she smiled.

"No...you don't." he said really looking at her for the first time in 12 years.

"Okay…tried of saying this but…what?" she asked seeing his stare.

"You let your hair grow."

"Yeah…so?" she replied insecurely moving her hand through the strands.

"It's nice." he said. "And I'm guessing a few new tattoos as well?"

"A few...wanna count 'em?" she hoped.

"No." he said knowing what it could lead to. "Especially not with the current situation."

With everything happening Jordan forgot about the one thing she wanted and needed to asked Danion.

"Why are you working for James?"

"Well...'didn't hesitate on that question, did we?"

"And you haven't answered it yet."

"It's complicated."

"How complicated can it be? You're helping James steal fairie land."

"The land is his."

"The OC's had that land for centuries."

"As did the Indians tribes across America and yet what happened there? They lost their land…died in a futile cause…and though I really enjoyed the legal maneuvering you did with those mercenaries there is still nothing you can do to keep James from getting that land."

"What else can he do?" she asked.

Danion's eyes widened to the thought of the trolls that were hired to attack the OC. More to the point that it was his idea to hire them in the first place which was strongly motivated by hatred to the OC because he thought Jordan was a fairie trick. Now that he knew the truth he was quickly regretting his actions but there was no turning back and he knew it.

"It doesn't matter." he said.

"The hell it doesn't…6 Gur-Fanng were killed. Why? How could you be working for James…money?"

Money?" he said insulted. "I don't need money and I wouldn't take any from James. You think I like working for that..."

He was going to say more that shouldn't be said but changed his mind with the frustration of the situation.

"Enough." he said turning his back to her. "Just go."

"Go...?"

"Yes…please go."

"What about you and me?"

There was a pause between them.

"There is no you and me... not anymore." he said to her with a coldness Jordan never felt from Danion. "Go home."

"Danion---"

"Go-Away." he ordered.

The tone in his voice echoed through her ears and crushed her heart...metaphorically of course but the pain was still quite real.

"Fine...I'll go away." she said in a slightly quivering voice.

She started searching her pockets for her keys. Fighting the tears that were forming in her eyes. 'I not gonna cry.' she told herself turning away from Danion so he wouldn't see her face. She finally found her keys but they slipped out her hand being caught in the pocket the way they do sometimes and fell to the floor behind her.

"Damn it." she said turning around to pick them up.

As she grabbed the keys she suddenly saw and felt Danion's fingertips on her hand.

When he heard the keys fall he bent down to pick them up for Jordan at the same time she did and didn't noticed each other until they made physical contact.

He looked at Jordan's face as her hair was slightly blocking her eyes where moisture was forming in the tear-ducts. He hurt her. He knew it. There were no words spoken as his hand was still touching hers', feeling her body temperature rise from his touch.

Jordan could feel her heart beating through her chest. The sound of it inside her body was so loud that she thought Danion could hear it which he could with those vampire ears. He moved his fingers up her hand where he saw the beginnings of her bracelet tattoo. Jordan looked down as Danion glided his fingertips over the skin of the tattoo. She closed her eyes to the sensation. It felt so good to have him touching her again after so long. Jordan opened her eyes to Danion's and asked with them…'So... what now?'"

Moments passed which felt like an eternity as Danion looked back at her.

"One." He said.

Why did he just say that he asked himself? He didn't have an answer but it was all Jordan needed to hear to grasp Danion's face in her hands to start softly kissing him. There was one… then two but by the third Jordan could feel Danion trying to pull away from her…she was not about to let that happen.

As he tried to move back she moved forward giving another kiss with each attempt he made. Jordan decided to move her hands from Danion's face and take a gentle but firm hold of his head to keep him in place… close to her.

The kisses became more intense as one from Jordan was able to push Danion down to the floor. She moved her hands down to his shoulders pinning Danion against the carpet. He took his hands and took hold of Jordan's wrist and the kissing stopped as the two looked at each other. Was Danion going to throw her off she thought as Jordan looked down at him. He looked up at her seeing the question in her eyes… the answer came a moment later when Danion released his hold on Jordan's wrist and put up the palm of his hands to show her that there wasn't going to be any resistance from him on what was about to happen.

She lowered herself down to kiss Danion again. Jordan then pulled away slightly and started playfully licking the tip of his nose. She then sat up straddling Danion as he laid on the floor and began to remove her jacket. Her arms were exposed from her short sleeve shirt and a curious look appeared on Danion's face. Jordan noticed the look and realized why Danion had it. He first thought the tattoos he saw were new added to the ones he remembered from Denver. Seeing now that those tattoos were gone Danion's mind flashed that maybe this was still a fairie trick… that this woman above him may not be Rail.

Jordan understood his confusion… how could he know about these new tattoos? How could he know about the variety of tattoos she got after she left Denver and right then and there she really didn't want to talk about the reasons that lead to why she had those tattoos removed.

She held opened her arms so Danion could get a clear view of the art that was across her skin. She smiled as she slightly rotated her arms showing the detail artwork. They were beautiful… not multicolored like the Denver tattoos but there was a tint of color to make the images pop to the observer's eye. Danion was admiring the designs on her arm but quickly loss focus when Jordan with one smooth motion removed her short sleeve shirt. As the shirt went passed her head Jordan's long hair fell back down passed her shoulders. She pushed the strains of hair away from her face that were blocking her view of him and when she had a clear look at him again Jordan was slightly taken back by the expression of Danion's face.

It was a look of awe… he had never seen her with long hair before and she looked amazing with it. He reached out and curled some strains of her hair between his fingers. Jordan then took hold of his hand and started caressing it with kisses. She then held his hand against her skin and guided it down to the center of her chest so Danion could feel her beating heart. It wasn't an attempt to turn him on but Jordan could feel beneath her that Danion was beginning to get there.

Jordan stood to her feet above Danion and proceeded to remove the rest of her clothing. She kicked off her boots and socks, and like her shirt, smoothly slipped out of her pants revealing the second half of her attractive two piece undergarments. Pretty as they were they soon were removed to reveal Jordan's more attractive nude body. She slowly turned her body in a circle so Danion could receive a full view of all her body art making his awe of her increase… as well as his 'excitement'.

Suddenly Jordan grabbed Danion by the shirt and jacket and lifted him off the floor. With no surprise from Danion Jordan was holding him a foot and a half off the floor. She then plodded him down on his feet and kissed him again as she started to unbuttoned his shirt. She moved her kisses down his neck to his chest and moved the kisses lower with each new opened button. Danion was a bit surprised with this as he half expected Jordan to simply rip his shirt off… than again he wasn't complaining.

Jordan began to unfasten his belt as Danion kicked off his shoes. She slipped her hands passed the two layers of clothes to the skin of Danion's hips and pushed down those layers to the floor so Danion could step out from them. Jordan still not losing contact with Danion's skin came up and pushed the upper clothes off his body. As his coat and shirt fell to the floor Jordan slowly stepped back so she could receive a full view of Danion's almost nude body. He felt rather ridiculous wearing nothing other than his socks and began to motion to take them off but was stopped by Jordan.

"Don't". She said.

Jordan was enjoying the image in front of her. The arms, the abs… just Danion himself but Danion could tell by the Jordan's smile that enjoyment was enhanced by the added factor of those sock.

"Seriously?" he asked.

"Ohhh... seriously!" she answered with werewolf eyes.

Jordan rushed towards Danion, wrapped her arms around him, and kissed Danion like there was no tomorrow. She then wrapped one of her legs around his waist to make sure this moment could last for as long as possible. Danion reached down and took hold of the upper thigh of Jordan's standing leg. As his fingers began to press into her skin Jordan lifted her other leg and locked both around Danion's torso.

Perspiration was starting to form in the pores of their bodies clearly showing how the heat between them was intensifying. It was then that Danion felt a small pinch of pain on his back. A second later he felt another. The pinches of pain grew in number until they stopped exactly at ten. Danion knew what was causing those points of pain he felt them before in Denver and didn't mind them... that is until Jordan's claws dug too deep into Danion's shoulder.

"Aaahh!" he cried breaking that marathon kiss with Jordan.

She had an obvious confused look on her face until Jordan spotted her blood-stained claws on Danion's shoulder.

"I'm sorry." She said with some embarrassment.

"Don't be…" he said pulling her body back close to him. "Let yourself go."

She immediately flashed back to that Denver night where Danion was not afraid or embarrassed to be with Jordan in her werewolf form. She always loved him for that and after twelve years there was no hesitation from him again, which only reconfirmed that love.

Another rush of pleasure went through Jordan's body as Danion started passionately kissing her neck. She instinctively dug her claws back into Danion causing him to give a grunt of pain but not breaking off those neck kisses. Jordan peeked down over Danion's shoulder and watched as her claws morphed back into hands. After twelve years Jordan had more control over her primal side in these situations. On that Denver night Jordan bared herself to Danion completely where she could be unafraid, unencumbered, and completely primal… but this night was different. She wasn't ashamed of her werewolf form but it wasn't the best way to express how sensual she wanted to be with Danion.

Jordan unwrapped her legs from around Danion as he began to carry her over to the bed. He carefully laid her top of the blankets and started kissing her naked skin. Her lips turned into a growing smile with each kiss and when those kisses centered onto a certain spot on Jordan's body her smile turned into a hard biting of her bottom lip. She then turned over to feel those continuing kisses on the other side of her body.

Danion started at the small of her back, moved up to each her shoulders blades, and held steady on the back of her neck. He reached out and took hold of Jordan's hand, their fingers began to interlock as both felt the pressure and pleasure of holding one another's hand. Jordan closed her eyes to fully engulf herself in the moment then another moment later her eyes opened in ecstasy as she could feel a penetrating pleasure in her body coming from Danion's body. The ecstasy level in both of them rose higher with each trust Jordan was receiving from Danion.

A change of positions found Jordan and Danion facing each other, Jordan again took hold of Danion's face in her hands as he looked down and saw an expression of both emotional and physical intensity in Jordan's face. She took hold of him with her legs and arms and pulled Danion towards her pressing their bodies together once again.

She could taste the perspiration off his neck and began slightly licking at it. It began to tickle and Danion let out small giggle, Jordan's ears peaked again at that giggle and knew she had to keep tickling him but very quickly the licking turned into small nibbling on Danion's neck.

There was no denying it… it was a turn-on to Danion causing him to increase his motion within Jordan and starting a circle of pleasure between them.

The more she nibbled the more he motioned and the more he motioned the more the nibbling continued. Round and round this went with both their bodies feeding off their passion for each other. Building and growing until finally that passion was released from Danion's body into hers' resulting in a climaxing howl from Jordan.

She looked at him. He looked at her. Their stares not breaking as they laid next to each other. Jordan just simply kissed Danion. What happened between them was better than the first time they were together in Denver. In the twelve years she believed that Danion was dead Jordan often thought about what she would say if she had one more moment with him. Her mind was swimming in emotions now that that moment was quite literary in front of her but with a tear forming in her eye one thought was very clear and Jordan had no hesitation in immediately telling Danion.

"You have no idea how much I've missed you." She said.

Well…no need to tell you what took place over the next 18 hours…not with imaginations as sick as yours(Frank) but quite honestly it was simply a passionate night between them in bed and when the sun came up to greet the new day a passionate day between them in bed.

The clock on the wall was saying it was just shy of 5:07 in the PM. Jordan had her head on Danion's chest, one arm around his neck, while the other arm was wrap around his torso. Every time Danion moved the slightest inch Jordan tightened her hold on him in saying, 'You're not going anywhere' as she was afraid he'd disappear if she let go him and that the last 18 hours didn't happen.

That it wasn't real.

For close to two hours Danion was looking up at the ceiling of his hotel room pondering this new development. He looked at her as she laid resting on him peacefully and beautiful but he made a decision and now needed to follow through with it. He tried to slip out of Jordan's grasp but like before she strengthened her hold.

"I'm not letting you go." she said with her eyes still closed as if she was sleeping.

"No…I'm letting you go." he said in an empty tone. He forcefully broke away from Jordan getting out of bed and using his free hand to tear her hand away from the one she was holding.

"What are you doing?" she asked watching Danion pick up her clothes in a heated frenzy.

"You're leaving." he said.

"Why?"

"Because I say so." he said grabbing her by the arm and pulling her out of bed.

There were shows of pain in Jordan's face as she felt pieces of glass from the broken picture frame going into her skin from Danion dragging her across the floor.

"What the hell are you doing?" she cried with obvious confusion.

"What we did last night was a mistake. You're leaving...Now!" he said tossing her clothes out the door and Jordan right behind them. "Don't come back...and if you know what's good for you stay away from the OC tonight."

He slammed and locked the door behind him leaving her naked on the hall floor. She started banging on the door demanding that Danion open up.

He didn't.

"We'll fuck you then!" she yelled putting on her clothes in the hallway.

Jordan stared at Danion's door perplexed, angry, and most of all hurt.

"What's wrong with you?!" she yelled again with one last bang at the door.

She left the hotel and hit the hood of her truck in anger. She wanted answers to the sudden 180 after last night. She thought back to those hours and how good it felt to be with Danion again and how wonderful it would feel to be with him from now on. Then hearing what he said as he threw her out of the room, 'What we did was a mistake'…It didn't feel like a mistake to her. 'Don't come back.' and then the last part, 'Stay away from the OC tonight.'"

Tonight?

Danion let something slip. Something was going down with the OC and clearly nothing good from Danion's tone. She got in truck and headed home to Keff who could warn the OC since Jordan couldn't tell any of the Gur-Fanng how she got this information.

Trolls.

For years people thought of trolls as tiny deformed men with pig knuckles for hands. The truth is trolls come in a variety of sizes from dwarfs, man size, and just plain big. They like to live in dark spaces. Caves, abandon buildings, and of course under bridges. Ever seen somebody living under a freeway overpass? Half the time it's a troll in disguise but no one notices because no one wants to notice the homeless.

Their strength also varies with size. The dwarfs are about as strong as a full-size male while the man-size are as strong as a werewolf and the just plain big ones...we'll they're just plain strong. More than enough muscle to handle the Gur-Fanng if they got in the way of earning that other half of a large amount of gold coins.

They already knew the location of the OC village that was tucked away in the backwoods in the center of a circle of grove trees away from the praying eyes of humans. Usually there was a clear line neither troll nor OC cross staying out of each other's territories…but the promise of gold can make you cross many lines.

They attacked the village from all sides destroying the small homes of the OC. The fairies scattered across the area trying not to be caught or killed by rampaging trolls. Then out of nowhere a horn sounded off and holes started opening up in the earth around the village. Immediately all the fairies drove into the holes leading underground and just as quickly as the holes opened up for the fairies they closed back up from the other side keeping the trolls from following.

Okay…here's some good troll info. The majority of them are not that bright. Example…as they were wondering what happened to all the fairies not one realized that they just walked into a trap. The sky rained with arrows hitting their marks with pin-point accuracy…unfortunately it wasn't going to keep them down. You see just like werewolves trolls have hyper-healing but unlike werewolves when the old adrenaline gets pumping the healing comes faster.

Word to the wise…hyper-healing and stupidity are two really bad combinations.

Then like the Calvary of the old west (of Hollywood). The Gur-Fanng came charging at the trolls in full werewolf mode. Many were holding their own against the man-size trolls while others were having problems with the dwarf trolls as they were piling on Gur-Fanng three or four to one. Even though they were healing fast the arrows inside them were not helping the trolls and were giving the Gur-Fanng the upper-hand in the battle...that is until re-enforcements arrived in a massive 10-foot troll named Grull.

He started slapping away Gur-Fanng throwing them from side to side like old toys. Another wave of arrows came firing down on him but they were just more annoying than painful. Suddenly one Gur-Fanng took a log and clocked the troll on the back of the neck.

No effect...and a really bad idea.

In response Grull grabbed the Gur-Fanng and put the werewolf in a massive bear-hug. The air quickly rushed out of the Gur-Fanng's lungs making him black-out and revert back to his human form of Craig Matters.

Other Gur-Fanng tried to help but some were still busy with other trolls or were brushed away by Grull as he increased his hold on Craig. Jordan being one of those werewolves got back up and quickly grabbed and clawed at the troll's hands trying to get him to let go of Craig to no avail. Her ear twitched at the sound of bones breaking inside of Craig. Jordan grabbed hold of the troll's fingers trying to pry them open only to have Grull laugh at her half-ass attempt to out match him in strength not noticing that her yellow werewolf eyes were starting to glow for a brief moment...red.

The next thing that happened was the cry of pain from Grull as Jordan broke his fingers.

Craig fell to the ground from being let go as Jordan held out the troll's arms by the broken fingers of each hand. In shocked and pain over what just happened Grull was a clear target for a boot in the face. Jordan then went under Grull and lifted him over her head and threw him 30 feet against a tree.

The other Gur-Fanng started pushing back the other trolls when someone cried, 'We got 'em…take cover! Take cover!!'. With that a new shower of arrows came raining down on the trolls.

Fire arrows.

The arrows being on target the trolls started catching fire. Even with hyper-healing the sensation of being set ablaze is not a pleasant one so the trolls started to run for their lives. Even Grull took off…not just because of the fire but because he didn't want to go another round with Jordan or any other werewolf who might be stronger than him.

Maybe trolls are not so dumb after all.

Cheers came echoing across the village as fairies came out from the reopened holes in the earth to see the last of the trolls running off. Suddenly rain started coming down on the village. The Gur-Fanng were confused since it didn't smell like rain that night then some noticed that the rain wasn't coming down pass the village limits.

Fairie magic.

They made it rain to put out the fires in and around the village. The next hour was determining the damage to the village, it's residents, and the Gur-Fanng.

"How is he?" Jordan asked with Kefflynn about Craig.

"Three broken ribs." a healer answered.

"Good." Keff said.

"Yeah…in a couple of hours they'll just be bruised." said Jordan.

"Thanks." Keff said to the healer.

"No. Thank him." Gerradenn said about Craig. "Thank all the Gur-Fanng. Without them we wouldn't have beaten the trolls so easily…but they'll be back."

"How do you know?" asked Keff.

"James knows he can't use humans to do his dirty work anymore so he used trolls so we can't do the same thing we did before."

"No worries…you came up with a plan for them tonight you'll come up with one to beat them tomorrow." said Keff.

"Well…I'm glad one of us is that confidence." said Gerradenn.

"Oh, come on everybody knows you're a shoe-in to be an Elder in 100 years." said Keff showing her admiration.

"A hundred years? I'm more concerned with the present and immediate future. Which doesn't look bright with that vampire being James's Lore connection." said Gerradenn.

"Cuse me?" Jordan asked over hearing the two fairies' conversation.

"I talked to a few Gur-Fanng…they caught a whiff of vampire on some of the trolls." Gerradenn said. "Probably hired them for James. Now we're right back where we star---. I'm sorry…someone calling for me…I gotta go."

As Gerradenn flew off Jordan looked at the damage of the OC village. Whole sections were destroyed as fairies looked at their former homes that they lived in for who knows how long.

"I'm sorry." Jordan said.

"For what? We came out of this pretty good…and no one died." said Keff.

"Your home..."

"Hey…I think everyone here's gonna agree that they rather be rebuilding houses than burying friends and family." Kefflynn said to an unresponsive Jordan. "You're thinking about him again…aren't you?"

"He knew this was gonna happen. He let this happen. Hell…if Gerradenn's right he probably helped set the whole thing up."

"I'm sorry." Keff said sitting on Jordan's shoulder trying to give some comfort to her friend.

"I don't know what's going on with him?"

"Don't beat yourself up about this J. It's just time to let go?"

"I can't…not after last night." she said.

"Last night? Last night?" Keff asked. "Hello…what about today when he threw you out, bare-ass, in the middle of a hallway."

"There's something I'm not seeing...something he's not telling me."

"Like he's not the same person you knew 12 years ago." Keff stressed.

But Jordan just stared ahead pondering everything...remembering the night before and the recent troll attack on the OC all the while caressing her bracelet tattoo under the sleeve of her jacket.

"I'm gonna see him again." Jordan said.

"J...no!"

"I have to know what's happening with him."

"And what if what's happening is he's just gone bad?"

Jordan turned to Kefflynn with a blank expression then grabbed a branch off the ground and broke it into a form of a stake.

"Then I'll stake this in his heart myself...happy?"

No..." replied Keff.

Jordan's blank expression turned to surprise from Keff's answer.

"...Because if you do that I think you'll die two minutes later of a broken heart."

A long silence came between them as Jordan thought about what Keff said. What if Danion had gone bad? What if she had to fight him or worse...kill him?"

No.

Things hadn't come to that...yet. If Danion had gone bad then why did he warn her about the attack? Because he cared…she hoped. Or maybe he didn't want to warn her at all. Maybe it was what she thought before…a slip and that maybe he wanted the village destroyed as much as James. The anxiety of not knowing was getting to Jordan which was not being missed by Kefflynn.

"Listen…you do what you think you need to do. Just be careful." said Keff. "I don't want you hurt by this guy anymore."

Jordan slightly nodded her head to acknowledged Keff's concerns.

"I'm gonna check on my folks…meet you later at home." said Keff.

"Okay."

"Hey…Cheer up. We won tonight and if you keep tossing trolls like you did we'll keep winning."

"Yeah… the Hulk's got nothing on me." Jordan joked.

"Didn't know Howlers were that strong." Keff said flying off.

"Neither did I."

The truth was they aren't and Jordan knew that as she was trying to pry Craig loose from Grull using all her werewolf strength to no effect. Then out of nowhere there were broken fingers and she was now the new world champion in troll tossing. 'What did it matter anyway?' she told herself. She saved Craig that was the important part so why look a gift horse in the mouth?

Or two.

You see the OC knew about the troll attack thus there was a plan to defend themselves. How? It wasn't Jordan or Keff I'll tell you. When Jordan got home from her night and day with Danion she told Keff everything thus her knowing about Jordan's bare-ass in the hallway including Danion's comment about staying away from the OC. They tried to work out a plan that would warn the OC of what was coming not knowing exactly what was coming while still trying to keep Jordan's secret. Then out of nowhere the phone rang putting out the word that trolls were going to attack the fairie village that night. In an instant the problem was solved. The OC were warned about the coming danger clearly with more information than Jordan had and everyone who was anyone was still in the dark about Jordan 'sleeping with the enemy' but the questions still itched at her on how the OC knew they were going to be attack that night?

"How indeed?" Danion said hearing the same question from the defeated trolls.

He had waited back at the trolls' cave expecting to hear the 'good news' that the fairies were ready to surrender their land.

He didn't get it.

"And the Gur-Fanng were there?" asked Danion.

"Yeah…they were waiting for us." a burned troll said.

"Whether they were ready for you or not wasn't my question. I knew there would be some resistance. Definitely from the OC…possibly the Gur-Fanng which would have made your job a lot harder. That's why you were there to tip the odds in our favor. Yet…you still come back beaten?" Danion said looking with disappointment at Grull.

"It wasn't my fault…" Said Grull. "That Howler was strong."

"Howler?" Danion asked.

"Yeah…she was not Gur-Fanng I could smell it."

"She?" Danion said closing his eyes knowing who 'she' was. "She's the one who broke your fingers?"

"Yeah…look what that dog did to me." said Grull holding out his healing fingers.

"Dog…huh? May I?"

Danion looked at Grull's hand so he could exam how a werewolf even of Jordan familiar intensity could break the fingers of a troll of three times her size and strength?

Seconds later there was a shout of pain as Danion re-broke Grull's fingers.

"Hmm…I guess it's possible." Danion said turning his back to ponder his next move.

"Uh…does this mean we don't get the rest of our gold?" a troll asked.

A yellow eye opened in Danion but went completely unnoticed by the trolls as Danion lashed out at that troll's face for his very untimely and stupid question.

"At this moment...no." Danion said calmly as the troll laid on his back with a bloodly face in pain. "But stand by...I may have other plans for you which involves more gold."

The other trolls laughed with greed at the prospect of more gold. Danion started to head out when he noticed that there was something in his hand. He looked down with a raised eyebrow at the sight that was rolling between his troll blood dripping fingertips

"I uh... think this is yours. Sorry." he said tossing back the eye that he ripped from the troll's face.

He came out of the cave walking a few yards to find a clearing to take off into the night skies. His anger was still boiling in him. An anger not just directed at the troll for failing but at himself for knowing why they failed. His want and need to get rid of Jordan at his hotel made him slip up and reveal, at least partially, the attack on the OC. Even though he came up with the idea about the trolls through anger there was still some logic behind it. Get the trolls to attack the fairies to show that a little thing like the law wouldn't stop James from getting their land. Danion was capable of getting other and more smarter Lore to work for James but the trolls were immediate cannon-fire and the message needed to be send immediately to give up their futile crusade…and not to use images of past loves against a certain vampire. But no doubt this latest victory had only strengthened they're resolve and things didn't get any better when a familiar light came flying towards him.

"Lee-Shannon." he greeted.

"Tonight didn't go as planned I see." she said.

"No...especially since you warned the OC beforehand!" cried Danion pinning the fairie against a tree between his two fingers.

"What are you talking about?"

"Please do not think me as stupid as a troll. From what I got from them, the OC were ready for them. It became real clear when the Gur-Fanng put them in a position where the OC could hit them with a brigade of fire-arrows…something very effective against trolls. Elves as a rule don't use fire-arrows in the forest because it might start a forest fire but if they knew they were dealing with trolls they could make up a plan to put them in a position where they could use fire-arrows with little to no threat of a forest fire." said Danion. "Now...only three people knew about the plan tonight. You, me, and James. I didn't tell. James wouldn't tell. So...that only leaves you."

"Killing fairies wasn't part of the plan." Lee-Shannon confessed knowing she was busted.

"Bad time to get a conscious here, Lee-Shannon," he said. "You, like me, are supposed to get those fairies off the land then you're suppose---"

"I know what I'm supposed to do."

"And yet you decide to play the good little fairie and warn the OC. The Consortia's not going to be very happy with that"

"Fuck 'em."

Her rather direct response brought an odd expression on Danion's face... an actual smile.

"Thank-you...I needed that." he said letting Lee-Shannon go from the tree. "And thank-you for correcting my mistake with the trolls."

"Really?" Lee-Shannon said with some confusion.

"I made that decision about killing OC in the heat of the moment over some...incorrect information but by the time I found out the truth it was too late to turn back. I'm honestly glad none of your people were hurt."

"Thanks." she said feeling the great 'warmth' of a vampire.

Ever since Danion saw Jordan again he been running on emotion.

Not good.

Not now.

It was time for him to get back in the mindset he was before he came to Jackson Point. Time to use his logic first and his emotions not at all.

How Vulcan of him.

He was refocused on the plan of getting the OC off their land so James could usher his way in and then put as much distance between him, Jackson Point, and someone else as quickly as possible.

From the dark recesses of his mind, a very disturbing place indeed with most Lore (but not half as bad as some human) he came up with a plan that was going to achieve all these goals in one giant stroke.

"Well...I hope it's better than your last plan." said Lee-Shannon.

"No one's going to die if that's your meaning... I hope" he said. "The Elders... I need to know who their offspring are."

"Why?"

There was no answer but anyone who had a two-digit I.Q. could see what was going to happen next.

"It could work." said James when he heard the new plan for getting the OC's land.

"Well...if it came down to protecting your land or protecting your children which one would you choose?" Danion asked then remembered who he was talking to. "Perhaps you're not the best example for that question. By having the Elders' Offspring we can force them to give up the land with no opposition."

"Brilliant in its simplicity, sir." said Davis to James. "I'm surprised you didn't think of it."

Immediately James gave a cold stare in saying, 'Shut-up, Davis', which Davis did.

"Why not just take the Elders themselves?" James asked.

"Trying to capture an Elder fairies is...difficult to say the least. Besides the Elders are the only ones who can officially surrender the land to you." said Danion. "Having their offspring will ensure that."

"So when do we do this…tonight?" asked James.

"No…if they're expecting another attack they'll figure it for tonight. Give them some breathing room…let them get relax then hit them again. I also need the trolls again for this which means..."

"More gold." said James. "You have it."

Danion was a little taken back by James's easy willingness to shell out more gold but shrugged it off knowing this would ensure the trolls' involvement.

"Well…they're in." said Danion.

"Yes…but are you sure you can even get to the Offspring? After last night they're bound to be guarded." said James.

"I plan to get the bulk of their forces including the Gur-Fanng away the OC village. Like you said 'after last night' they'll want to keep the fighting away from there.

"How?"

"They're going to attack us." said Danion.

"Excuse me?" James asked with a perplexed look.

Danion used the objects on James's desk as an example in his plan. The OC would attack the trolls in one place away from the village while a smaller group of trolls would go in and take the Offspring with little resistance.

"How will they know where you are to attack you?" asked James.

"They'll know." Danion told James not telling him the part of Lee-Shannon telling the OC about the attack and her telling the OC they should hit them before the trolls reach the village.

Danion's only concern was the trolls themselves. Would the ones who were supposed to distract the OC from the village keep them busy enough so the others could nab the Elder Offspring or just until they felt they earned their gold. As for the other trolls…Danion wasn't nice about it, he just felt they would screw things up if he wasn't there to make sure things went right. He needed to be at both sites to make sure the plan went off without a hitch but that was impossible.

"I think a solution has just arrived." James said looking passed Danion.

Danion turned and was shock to see a person he thought had died.

"Major?" Danion asked.

"He showed up sometime last night." said James. "A little worse for wear but in one piece."

The Major was brought up to speed on things by James after his team's total defeat at the claws of the Gur-Fanng. He was then told Danion's plan and his dilemma with the trolls that would distract the OC

"I'll take the trolls to fight the Gur-Fanng. I got some major payback for those fleabags." the Major said cocking his 9mm loaded with silver bullets. "Which is gonna go right to the center of their skulls."

"No...I'll go with those trolls. The werewolves will be extra motivated to fight if I'm there...giving you a better chance to get the Offspring." said Danion.

"What makes you so special?" the Major asked.

Danion looked at the Major slightly perplexed then it flashed on him that the Major still didn't know that Danion was a vampire.

"It's not important, but they will stay and fight." promised Danion.

"Well...if everything is set I'll have the housekeeper make us brunch. She's a wonder I may hire her fulltime." said James. "Major I'm sure after your ordeal you're definitely in the mood a hearty meal...and what are you in the mood for Danion?"

"Sleep actually." he said. "Dawn's already passed and I've been up most of the night."

"Of course...there are plenty of rooms upstairs." said James.

"Here's fine." said Danion. "Soft couch. Shades are already down. Just switch off the lights and it's nice and dark. Easier to sleep that way."

"Fine. Wake you up...when?" asked James knowing Danion would be stuck inside until the sun went down.

"When I wake up." said Danion.

James, the Major, and Davis left the office while Danion got comfortable on the couch. Even with the lights off he had a clear view the room through his night-vision but things went completely black as he closed his eyes to go to sleep. Time passed. Who knows how much but James's office door opened and closed and Danion was seen clearly through Jordan's night-vision. She snuck into the house and sniffed Danion out. She walked closer and saw him sleeping peacefully in the dark. Her mind suddenly flashed to a moment back in Denver and couldn't resist the urge coming over her.

Jordan watched as the famous brooding frown on Danion charged into a smile from her kissing him on the cheek. She kissed him again and the smile grew bigger, increasing Danion peaceful sleep.

Have you ever been sleep and suddenly you start to feel really good? Now your mind knows that sensation isn't coming from a dream but from the outside world...so you obviously wake up to see the cause of it.

"What are you doing here?" he said to Jordan with a second shocked tone and expression of the day.

"We have to talk." she said. "I waited at the hotel but when dawn came I figured you be here to sleep the day out."

"You must have some sort of death wish coming here." he said.

Not the first time he said that to her Jordan remembered and the reason was the same as before, curiosity with the little added motivation of love.

"Trolls. The bastards send trolls against us and you knew about it. You let it happen."

"Yes and no." Danion stated. "Yes...I did know about the trolls. Yes...I did let it happen. But no...James didn't send them...I did."

"W-Why?"

"I think that would be obvious." he said.

There was a cold silence between them as Jordan shook her head at Danion wondering and dreading if Keff was right. Did Danion just go bad?"

"Now that this information is out in the open I hope it will be the final nail that convinces you that what's gone is gone…and that it's never coming back." Said Danion.

"If that's true then why did you warn me to stay away from the OC?" she asked.

"I made a slip. Nothing more nothing less, you shouldn't see anything in it. Now it's time to face facts and move on with your happy little life."

"My life hasn't been that happy in 12 years." said Jordan looking at Danion to express the answer of why she hadn't been that happy.

She reached out her hand to caress Danion's face only to have it slapped away as he turned his back to her.

"Then I strongly suggest you try harder in making it happy." he said.

"'Had a good start two nights ago."

"Like I said before…that was a mistake." he said. "A mistake I'm really---"

Suddenly the room was hit by a rectangular light from the open door of James's office by Davis.

"Mr. Danion? I thought I heard voices---"

"Immediately he saw Jordan who greeted him with yellow eyes and a primal growl. Davis got so spooked he cried out and tripped over his own feet. He scammered on all fours trying to get back to his feet to tell James about the intruder.

"I believe it's time for you to leave now." said Danion. "The leader of the mercenaries, the Major, survived your little surprised attack on his unit. Needless to say he wants revenge and will use silver bullets to get it."

Jordan hearing that started to leave but then something came to her. Something crazy. Something that could get her killed…but if it could prove something it was worth the risk.

"No." she said.

"What?" he asked turning to look at her.

"I'm not leaving. You're not going to let them shoot me."

"Well…that's a big risk you're taking especially with a bulletproof vest."

"I'm not wearing a vest." she said lifting up her shirt to show her naked torso.

Danion's eyes slightly widened at the sight but like before he shrugged it off.

"'Wouldn't have mattered anyway…the Major is aiming for the head now. It does the job just the same." he said.

Both of their enhanced hearing could pick up Davis leading James and the Major down the hall. Their arrival being immediate it was a battle of wills as both did nothing towards the situation. Jordan staying put waiting for the Major and Danion doing nothing to try to protect her.

"Why are you doing this?" he asked her.

"Just remembering a rooftop in Denver…at sunrise." she said hoping the memory would spark something in Danion. "You did something crazy to get me to say I still cared…now I'm doing something just as crazy to get you to say the same thing."

"This way! Hurry! Hurry!" cried Davis to James and the Major.

The three were less than 20 feet away from James's office. The seconds to their arrival seemed to stretch out to forever as Danion looked at Jordan with her face showing a look of conviction of not moving. Her heart was beating like a drum over what may or may not happen in the next few moments and it was a sound which Danion could clearly hear through her chest.

"Outta the way!" the Major cried to Davis pulling out his 9mm.

The cocking of the gun echoed through Danion's ears making him suddenly grab Jordan by the jacket to pull her close to him.

"Get it through your thick skull…I don't care anymore." he stated very clearly.

Then with no regard Danion threw Jordan through the window as the Major came into the room to take his shot. She landed outside the house with shattered pieces of glass around her. Danion quickly moved out of the way of invading sunshine as the Major went towards the window to see if he could still get shot at Jordan. He saw her

heading to the woods and took aim at her but was stopped by Danion.

"Save your ammo." he said. "You'll need it for later if you run into anymore...Gur-Fanng."

"Who was that?" James asked.

"I don't know." Danion lied. "A spy. An assassin."

"Did she find out anything?" James asked.

"No." Danion said moving into the hall to more avoid the sunlight from the broken window.

"Are you sure?" asked James.

"Very." said Danion.

"Good…the last thing we need now is another screw up." said James.

"Agreed." said Danion.

"How did you do that?" asked the Major.

"Do what?" asked Danion.

"That was a werewolf…and you throw it out the window like it was nothing." the Major said looking at Danion.

Danion and James looked at each other for an explanation.

"How did you do that?" the Major repeated now suspecting that there was more to Danion.

"Quick answer, Major... I'm a vampire." said Danion with no hesitation. "That's how I know about werewolves, trolls, and fairies. I'm a part of the Lore."

James looked at Danion and was stunned by his candor when before he wanted the mercs to know nothing about him.

"Or...another explanation would be that the werewolf jumped through the window." said Danion staring at the Major. "That's a more reasonable explanation. I mean…I couldn't have really thrown a werewolf through a window unless you honestly believe that crap about me being a vampire.?"

"R-Right." Said the Major. "Must've been seeing things. I'm gonna go check the perimeter."

As the Major left James looked at Danion knowing he just Jedied the Major.

"Nice trick." he said.

"Comes in handy." said Danion.

"Let's hope tomorrow's plan is just as easy."

"Indeed."

As for Jordan…going through the window caused a lot of cuts and scrapes but nothing that wouldn't be gone in an hour. She laid in the shade against a tree away from the brightness of the sun that was stinging her eyes. She thought back to the last thing Danion said to her. Though his words were clear his actions screamed otherwise and relieved any doubts about Danion to her.

"Don't care anymore?" she said with a small laugh. "Bullshit."

Craig Matters waited on the third floor of the Murdock Hotel waited for Danion.

Now you're asking…'What the fuck?!'

Good question.

It was earlier that same day that Craig went to see Jordan. He wanted to personally thank her for saving his butt from that 10-foot troll. He turned the corner of the hall and was about to knock on the door, when he heard Kefflynn yelling 'Are you insane?!'.

"He threw you through a frickin' window!" Keff screamed to Jordan.

"To save me." said Jordan. "I'm sure of it."

"Well let's hope the next time he wants to save you there's no gasoline and matches around."

"That's not funny."

"Wasn't meant to be." said Keff.
"J…Danion has told you twice that it's over. Now I'm as romantically hopeless as the next fairie but you're acting like one of those girls we see in a soap opera. Remember…the ones we swore to beat the crap out of if we ever met them in real life. I'm sorry J but some things are just plain clear and you need to get that through your head."

"Second person to tell me that today." said Jordan. "Well…if it makes you happy I probably would've been convinced if he let me be shot."

Keff looked at her friend shaking her head at Jordan's refusal to accept the obvious.

But it wasn't obvious…not to her.

"But he didn't." said Jordan. "He threw me out that window before that... Major could get off a shot and I heard him as I running away, 'Save your ammo' he said. He didn't want me to get shot."

"'Save your ammo?" asked Keff. "For what?"

"I don't know. All that matters is that Danion wanted to keep me safe."

"And he does this by throwing you through a window?"

"He did that for two reasons. One…to cover himself with James."

"You hope." Keff said still skeptical.

"Two…to convince me that he really didn't care anymore." said Jordan.

"How do you know that's not truth?"

"Because if you knew anything about werewolves and vampires he would have let me be shot…a lot."

"I still can't believe you were dating a vampire." said Keff.

Eyes widened on Craig upon hearing the 'Big secret'.

As for Jordan and Kefflynn there was a mild silence between them over the Danion situation. Jordan took a deep breath then started smelling something. It was fresh, slightly moist, and floral. She turned around and saw a bouquet of flowers on the kitchen table.

"Who sent these?" Jordan asked

"Craig. Remember him? Cute guy. Really likes you. Doesn't throw you through windows." Keff expressed. "He sent you those to 'Thank-you' for last night. Big time hard on for you…just wanna point that out again."

"Jesus…Keff how many times do I have to tell you Craig and I are just friends. That's it. Nothing else is going to happen between us...ever. I'm in love with---"

"Danion," Keff finished.

"Yes." she said in a tone which had no doubt in it. "Maybe I should just tell you why this is so important to me."

Craig walked away from the door at that point. The old 'just friends' line. He heard it once before but always hoped, as we all do, and now there was a new element.

Danion.

A vampire?

This couldn't be possible. A werewolf in love with a vampire? It was something that couldn't be true but Jordan said 'Yes' to Keff saying Jordan loved Danion…and now of course he had to see this Danion for himself. What could he have, a vampire, that could make a werewolf, the ancient enemy, fall for him with such devotion in her voice. Like anyone else filled with jealously he needed to know but what I want to know…as I'm sure some of you are wondering…how did he know what hotel Danion was at?

It wasn't hard to sniff out Danion's room. Even with housekeeping the stench of the House Vampire could be smelled through the door even with Danion not being there. Also…Craig could smell the scent of Howler. Jordan was here he told himself and with another good whiff he smelled something else and instantly knew what happened in Danion's room. This didn't make things better as the green-eyed monster festered in Craig until Danion's inevitable arrival.

Seriously? Honestly? Really didn't see this not happening.

"Danion." Craig said not needing to ask if Danion was Danion with one good whiff.

Danion sized up Craig and knew immediately that he was a Gur-Fanng but how he knew his name, why he was there, and how he knew Danion was at that hotel was still a mystery.

"What's between you and Jordan?" demanded Craig.

Though surprised by the question Danion instantly knew that Craig was someone who wanted to be the object of Jordan's affection which explained why he was there.

"Nothing." said Danion. "There is absolutely nothing between us."

"Don't give me that crap. I know what...happened here."

The mere thought of 'it' was not pleasing to Craig.

"What happened here...is none of your business."

"I'm making it my business." Craig said grabbing Danion by coat collar.

"I'm sorry…your name is?"

"Craig. Craig Matters." he answered surprised that Danion was asking.

"Well Mister…Matters? Some advice…" said Danion. "Attempted suicide does not impress Rai--- Jordan. It will make her come a runnin' but in the end…it just pisses her off. So please…paws off!"

Danion slapped Craig's hand off his coat as Craig responded with yellow eyes focused on Danion's throat.

"Heel. Do you really want to do this in the middle of a hallway? Kinda the main reason I chose a public hotel." Said Danion.

Craig succumbed the logic.

"Listen to me very carefully Mister Matters. Obviously… you want to have a relationship with Jordan. Go for it with my blessing. Now do us both a favor and leave me alone because right now I'm under a lot pressure to get a job done. No prizes for you if you guess what."

"Getting the OC's land."

"Yes…and you coming here and pushing me for answers to something that again is still none of your business is really pissing me off…and I've noticed of late, Craig, that I've had some trouble controlling my temper. That's not a good thing." Danion stressed. "Now…go away."

Craig backed off. Much as his male ego wanted to get into it with Danion he knew that it wouldn't change anything with Jordan and why make things more hectic with everything that was going on. So he started to walk away only to be stopped by Danion.

"Craig" he said. "What exactly is your relationship with Jordan?"

"It's none of your business." Craig said with a sarcastic irony.

"True enough" Danion said. "But at the very least you are her friend. So I hope as her friend that the private knowledge you have required about me and Jordan won't become public among the Gur-Fanng for any reason such as jealously and or pain of being rejected."

"I don't know what you're talking about."

"I hope so Craig. Jordan has made a pretty good life for herself here. With the history between vampires and werewolf that life could easily disappear. That's something I really don't want to see happen." Danion said shoving Craig and pinning him against the wall.

"Because if that was to happen…Craig..."

Danion finished his sentence with glowing red eyes making the point clear to Craig. There were no worries Craig was going to tell anyone even before Danion's threat but the threat itself brought out something in Craig. Guys understand it. When someone pushes and threatens you…you react to show you're no wimp. I know ladies…why do us men need to be so macho…aka jerks?

Simple answer...we're guys.

"You threatening me?" Craig asked knowing the answer.

"Yes."

"Good." he growled with yellow eyes slapping Danion's hand away then charging at him in full werewolf mode.

When Jordan and Kefflynn went to answer the knocking at their door Jordan got a good whiff and grasped at the scent of the House Vampire on the other side.

"Danion." she said opening the door to discover Craig over Danion's shoulder with a great many bruises across his face and body as Danion came inside and dumped Craig on the couch.

"He knows." Danion told Jordan.

"What? How?" she asked.

"He was listening through the door earlier to you and your roommate…that's how. He started asking questions…there was shoving, and then he confessed all including where you lived. Of course, this was before I broke his jaw." said Danion.

"What the hell did you do that for?" said Keff hovering over Craig to access the damage.

"One…he said the wrong word to me. Two…it keeps him from talking." said Danion.

"Craig wouldn't have told anyone about us." said Jordan.

"You sure about that?"

"Yes."

"He's not looking too good here." Keff said about Craig.

"He'll heal." Danion said. "And think twice about telling the Gur-Fanng about us."

"What makes you think he would tell?" asked Jordan.

"Why take the chance. Besides I made it real clear that it wouldn't be a good idea to ruin things for you here."

"Meaning?" she asked Danion.

"Meaning?" Danion said as if the question had to be asked. "Do you know what the Gur-Fanng would do to you if they found out you were involve with a vampire?"

"Yeah I do know but that's my problem…you don't care anymore remember?"

"Of course I care---"

And right there the kid betrayed himself. Hell…he gave himself away the moment he threatened Craig to protect Jordan. He closed his eyes to Jordan's victorious smile. She looked at Keff who gave a slight nod to acknowledge that Jordan was right about Danion.

"Damn it." he said storming out of the apartment.

"Take care of him." Jordan said to Keff about Craig as she rushed after Danion.

She followed him up to the roof where Danion was about to take off into the air.

"Stop!" she yelled out to him.

"Keep your voice down other werewolves live here." he said tapping his ear to remind her of their enhanced hearing.

Jordan got quiet and just stared at Danion. You know that stare guys, when your lady wants you to confess something...immediately.

"What?" Danion asked knowing her request but playing ignorant to it.

So Jordan intensified her stare.

"What? What?! What do you want me to say?" he cried nearly forgetting that there were other werewolves living in the building.

There was a silence from Jordan looking into Danion's eyes. There was an unwillingness in them to her that made Jordan come to a sudden realization.

"Nothing." she said. "I don't want you to say anything. I don't know why you're acting like this...I don't care---No that's a lie I do care. I just don't wanna... I just don't want to do this anymore. I going back down to check on Craig."

She turned around and started to head back to the roof entrance of the building but not before she had to say something.

"Y'know whether you admit it or not you gave yourself away down there." she said not looking at him because it was too painful. "But I guess that doesn't mean anything, right? Maybe the other night was a mistake."

If he just let her go it would have been over. She would have walked away and never looked back and it would have been the way Danion wanted it. No more complications. He could focus on the job and get the 'hell out of Dodge'. All he had to do was let her keep walking.

Come on people...this is a love story.

"It wasn't a mistake." he said.

Jordan stopped in her tracks and turned back to him.

"What?" she asked.

"It wasn't a mistake." he repeated. "What happened the other night happened because I wanted it to happen. I just shouldn't have let it happen. But you were there...so close...warm...and beautiful…I just…"

Danion shook his head knowing that night and day with Jordan was wrong but at the same time was sooo right.

"It was still a mistake how I let it happen but not a mistake that it did happen." he said looking at her.

Jordan walked up to Danion and tried to kiss him only to have him pull away.

"Please don't" he said.

"Why…because if we start we won't want to stop?"

That was the answer. More to the point Danion not wanting to stop if they started but Jordan didn't care and took Danion by the head and kissed him. It was a sensual locking of the lips lasting forever and yet not enough.

"No." he said breaking the kiss.

"Yes." she said resuming it.

"We can't do this." he said pulling away from her.

"Why?" she asked in understandable frustration.

"A lot because of what your grandmother told me 12 years ago. You do deserve to grow old with someone. Walking in the sun. Having kids. You do want kids, don't you?"

"Yes!" she smiled with a brightened face.

Suddenly it hit her. When Keff asked the question, Jordan hesitated. Now when Danion asked the same question there was a quick response. It wasn't that Jordan didn't want kids right away or someday. She just didn't realize until right there that she wanted those kids with one person in mind…Danion.

"How am I supposed to give you that?" he said to her with a disappointed face. "Also there are…things you don't know about and if they were ever to come to light I extremely doubt you would feel the same way about me."

"What things?" she asked.

Danion shook his head 'No'. He wasn't going to tell but she knew.

"James." she said. "Screw James. I don't care about James. I care about us...about you."

"And I care about you...obviously. That's why I broke 'lover boy's' jaw back there to keep him from talking."

Jordan heard the tone of jealously in Danion's voice when he called Craig 'lover boy'. She shamefully had to admit to herself that she liked it. Why? Girls always like it when their guys get a little jealous. It means that they worry about losing their girl to another guy. Did that mean Danion still considered Jordan to be his girl?

Definitely something to be happy about.

"You've made a good life here for yourself. You deserve it and I don't want you to lose it because of me" he said rising into the air to fly away. "Y'know as crazy as it was for Craig to confront me he did it because he cares about you. Good fighter too…probably will make a great mate and protector for someone even though she doesn't need protecting... most of the time. Someone to grow old with…walk in the sun with...and have kids with. Think about it."

She watched as he turned to fly away knowing that Danion was trying to point her affections to Craig. A noble endeavor but useless as Jordan jumped into the air on to Danion's back.

"No!" she shouted. "I need to tell you something."

She had to tell him what she wanted to say and was not going to let him go until he heard it.

"What good is it going to---"

"It's important." she said. "Just put us back down on the... roof?"

They both looked and were mildly shocked to see that what Jordan thought was 6 or 7 feet in her jump turned out to be a good 25 feet in the air. It was quickly forgotten as Danion landed Jordan back on the roof. He looked at her in silence wondering what she could say that could do any good for either of them and the entire situation.

"I love you."

A good start.

"I didn't realize how much till I saw you alive again." She said.

Technically vampires are undead but you get the picture.

"When I thought you were dead I kept asking for one more chance…one more day…one more hour with you so I could tell you how much I loved you and as time went by and I knew it wasn't going to happen. I went through a really really bad rabbit hole. Some days were good. A lot of them were bad. A few guys here and there…all assholes. Then I just hit rock bottom which I **REALLY** don't wanna talk about, but when I'd did I just finally asked what the hell was I doing to myself? So like a stupid talk show I remade myself. Took out the piercing, got rid of the my old tatts and got new ones, and headed up north to make a new start. But even after that I couldn't completely move on from you. Truth is I don't think I ever really tried."

She pulled back her right sleeve and showed Danion her bracelet tattoo.

"I wanted it to look like the one you gave me remember?" she asked.

"Yes."

She pointed to the hidden designs of the tattoo. It was in an old fairie language that few read anymore to better to keep her past a secret but she knew what the symbols meant and told Danion the exact meaning behind them…

'FOREVER-LOVE-MY-NIGHT-MAN.'

Danion stared at the tattoo not knowing what to say. He too had some bad periods in his life after he left Denver thinking Jordan was dead. Like her he didn't want to talk about them and that just made him come back to his mission towards the OC.

"I have to go." he said.

"Where…back to James?" she asked. "You said it isn't about money…then what is it? Does he have something on you?"

"He thinks…but no."

"Then why are you working for him?"

"Because I quite honestly don't have a choice in the matter."

"You have a choice. You always have a choice. I mean you could have turned Sal into the Consortia but you didn't---"

And that was it…she finally figured it out when she looked in Danion's face about the Consortia.

"I can't be this fucking stupid." she said closing her eyes to what she thought she should have known in the first place. "You working for the Consortia again."

"Yes."

"Why would the Consortia want to help James take the OC's land?"

"You don't ask too many questions when dealing with the Consortia. Actually…when it comes to the Consortia you shouldn't ask questions at all."

"Danion, if the Consortia is helping James, the OC don't have a chance."

"Them wanting James to have that land has nothing to do with helping him." he said then immediately cringing his face. "I've said too much and you know too much. Don't let anyone…ANYONE know that you know they're involved because if they find out both our lives won't be long lasting."

"Wait…maybe there something we could do like the last time."

"It wouldn't work." he said.

"Why not?"

"It just wouldn't." he said to her.

The stress of his voice told Jordan that Danion was hiding something. Something he couldn't or wouldn't tell her as he floated back up into the air. He turned to fly away only to turn back around to face her again.

"What's going to happen next was my idea…" he said "…but I swear to you I won't let it go too far."

And with that he took off into the dark skies. The first time Jordan found out about a plan against the OC it was a slip of the tongue, now Danion deliberately told her that something was coming.

Why?

We all do things for a reason even when we don't know why or can't or won't admit it to ourselves. Why did Danion give Jordan the heads up knowing full well that it would ruin James's plan…and more importantly the Consortia's?

Come on kids...I know you're not idiots here.

South America.

Brazil before Jackson Point.

Danion entered his hotel suite and immediately felt the presents of another House in the room.

"Hello Walsh."

"Danion. I got good news for you."

"They're bringing back Murder She Wrote."

"Even better." said Walsh. "It's possible that very soon you'll be out from the employment of one Derrick James."

"At long last." Danion said with a sigh of relief.

"As you know James has wanted to build a cooperate Camelot for his business empire."

"Yeah…he bought some land in Canada. As soon as the forest is cleared away he'll start building.

"Yes...but the problem is that the forest he's trying to clear away belongs to a group of OC...Fairies to be exact."

"Are you serious?" Danion asked with a laugh. "He's actually trying to build something on fairie land?"

"Gets funnier. This group of OC have Gur-Fanng helping them."

"An Alliance. Well he must be having a good 'ole time."

"Exactly...and as soon as you're done with the business down here he'll be calling you up there to deal with things."

"But of course...I won't be helping him." said Danion.

"No...you will do whatever is takes to make sure he gets that land."

"Excuse me?" Danion asked surprised by what he just heard.

We want him to get the land from the fairies." said Walsh. "More to the point we want him to take it in the sense of stealing it."

"Steal…from Fairies? That's insane do you know what they'll do to him?"

Walsh looked at Danion expressing that he knew exactly what would happen.

"Ah…" understood Danion. "What's the plan?"

"Simple. James steals the land from the Fairies. They curse him. He needs to get the curse removed."

"And I tell him about a powerful 'group' that can pull it off." said Danion.

"Correct. We've been looking for this opportunity for a long time even before we infiltrated you into his organization."

"And the glee for the last two years has been ooh soo wonderful." Danion said not hiding his sarcasm.

"You only have yourself to blame for why you are indebted to us again and working for James." said Walsh.

"Yes…as you constantly remind me but let me say this…even if James gets the land, which is more than likely he will. There's no guarantee that the OC will curse him…killing him would be a lot easier."

Okay...Curses 101. Much to the disappointment of fans of T.V. Witch shows curses are not that easy to place on people. Yeah, you can still place small ones on people but they don't really make a big impact and are easily reversible. Now the big curses...the really good ones that last for generations and that fairy tales come from, those are the ones that need a lot of feeling behind them.

Passion.

Anger.

Hate.

Something that focuses that energy into one central point. In this case...one Derrick James stealing the land that the OC have inhabited for centuries. Yeah, I know...why not just curse James in the first placed and stop him before he gets started? The problem is for a curse to be place on someone they actually have to commit the act you curse them for first. Though James legally owned the land the OC and the Gur-Fanng kept him from fully possessing it...thus negating the curse.

"Already thought of" Walsh said glancing pass Danion.

Danion turned around and for the first time came face to face with Lee-Shannon.

"This is Lee-Shannon. She is going to go ahead of you to Jackson Point as an official member of the Consortia." said Walsh.

"To help?" said Danion.

"No…to tell them to leave for their own survival and the good of Lore from being exposed." said Lee-Shannon. "They won't of course…and when James does take, the land with your help, I will suddenly become very OC and lead them in the direction of a curse."

"A fairie betraying other fairies." Danion said. "Doesn't happen too often. In fact… almost never. The results I hear are quite...unpleasant."

"Lee-Shannon's been told the bigger picture in this and agrees it needs to be done. Even though I'm sure her personal feelings are telling her otherwise." said Walsh.

"The bigger picture being you want James cursed by the OC so the Consortia can have him by the preverbal 'balls' for something in the future that I'm not privy to…nor want to be but if it gets me away from James and makes up for Boston I'm in…even if it means I have to deal with werewolves again." Danion said looking at Walsh who knew the story behind that last statement.

He responded by motioning Lee-Shannon to the side and led Danion out to the hotel balcony and speaking in a low tone so the fairie wouldn't hear him.

"I know you still have issues dealing with werewolves but get over it." Said Walsh "James has hired mercenaries to deal with the Gur-Fanng. That alone could end this by next week so being distracted by the past will only delay things."

"Understood." he agreed with Walsh.

"Speaking of James...the other matter?"

"I can neither confirm or deny."

"After two years?"

"Yes…after two years the word is still 'Maybe'."

"Fine…let's just focus on the task at hand." said Walsh. "Finish the business you have to do here for James then head up north to put the plan in motion."

"And if there's any problems?"

"We'll contact you."

"Of course…since I can't ever contact you."

"Keeps you're cover better intact." said Walsh. "Besides if everything goes as plan you won't be needing a cover for much longer."

"If everything goes as plan." Danion said in the tone of 'Famous last words'.

"You worry too much. What could happen?"

"Anything and everything."

Walsh thought about it for a moment then answered.

"Anything indeed."

Back in Jackson Point.

Danion lead the trolls to the prearranged spot where he knew the OC and the Gur-Fanng would attack thanks to the confirmation from Lee-Shannon. Everything went as planned as the Gur-Fanng charged at them in full werewolf mode. Elf-arrows filled the air…many of them trying to find their way into Danion's heart. He fought off a lot of Gur-Fanng trying his best not to do any 'permanent' damage because one of them could have been a close friend of Jordan's.

When he turned around to face yet another werewolf he prepared to defend himself when he saw 'her' eyes change from yellow to Caribbean blue. Jordan made a motion with her eyes then charged at Danion tackling him away from the sight of the other Lore.

"I knew you'd show up sooner or later." he said. "There still time for you to get some distance from this."

"You mean walk away?" she asked going back to human form. "I will when you will."

"I mean protecting yourself. By tomorrow the OC will surrender their land to James with no resistance or hesitation."

"How do you---What have you done?"

"Nothing you know and no one can accuse you of knowing." he said to her then slowly taking her by the shoulders. "It's over. You and me…it's over."

She tried to say something but he stopped her before she could.

"It's-over." he repeated. "It has to be. Too much time has gone by and too much has happened. To you...to me. You've made a life here with the Gur-Fanng. You can still have it after this is over but me I'll still be in debt with the Consortia and that just plainly means we can't ever be together again"

"Then run away." she said.

"Can't…they'll find me."

"You don't know that. Sal ran away and they never found her."

"But they will find me" he said. "Besides I couldn't runaway right now even if I wanted to."

"Why?"

"Reasons." he answered. "Reasons that I can't and really don't want to explain on why I cannot runaway. And as much as I love you Jordan there is nothing you can say or to change that."

"Marry me."

Okay…that was something.

Danion was struck speechless as he looked into Jordan's eyes that were screaming, 'I am serious'. He was so shocked by her proposal he could only manage to spit a small perplexed laugh with the obvious.

"What?"

"Marry me. We leave right now…both of us. We find a little church--- Justice of the Peace and we don't look back. We don't ask ourselves what happened after we leave…we don't even think about it. We just go." she said.

"Just like that…Just take off?"

Jordan responded with a slightly reluctant nod.

"Well we both know that's not going to happen." he said. "That was one of the reasons you broke up with me in Denver because you didn't want to choose between me and your pack. Now you're saying you're going to leave this pack and the friends you've made in the OC…that you'll honestly not going to constantly wondered what happened after we would leave? To the OC…the Gur-fann---"

"Of course I'll wonder about it damn it! I'll always wonder about it and I'll probably feel guilty about it for the rest of my life but I would still do it if it means I could be with you." said Jordan. "Marry me."

Jordan stared at him with her blue eyes desperate for an answer to come immediately. Danion stared back at her with his face filled with mixed emotions. His mouth opened and closed but no words were coming out. Finally…he closed his eyes to take a moment. He opened them again and was about to answer when a troll and Gur-Fanng appeared in the distance fighting. Danion took hold of Jordan and hid behind a tree to keep out of sight. As the two watched the troll and Gur-Fanng fight they suddenly noticed the two combatants were moving oddly slow like a movie in 'slow-mo'.

"What's wrong with them?" said Jordan.

Danion didn't have a clue as he watched the Gur-Fanng and troll shift from slow-motion to fast-forward. The two moved at enhanced speed and Danion noticed they didn't seemed to realize it. Then as if someone hitting the rewind bottom on the remote the troll and Gur-Fanng started moving in reverse. Every move tracked back from when they first came on the scene then they started all over again showing no sign of knowing what just happened to them.

"Damn it." Danion said looking at the ground beneath them in disbelief over his discovery. "That's it. Shit…that's why James want's the land so badly. That's why the OC is fighting so hard. It's a Nexus!"

"What?"

"It's a fucking nexus."

"No." Jordan said. "No way…the OC woulda told the Gur-Fanng they had a nexus."

"If you had a nexus in your back yard would you tell anybody?" said Danion. "If this is what James is really after---Crap! I have to get word to the Consortia."

"Why?"

"The Consortia controls most of the nexuses on Earth. There's no way they'll going to let someone like James have one for himself."

"You really think he knows there's a nexus here?"

After all the money he's put in…willing to put in for this whole thing. Oh yeah…he knows." said Danion. "Don't worry…this is good news for the you. The Consortia will stop James and the OC will keep their land. Though…they'll probably have to negotiate their rights to it with the Consortia."

He was about to take off to try to get a line on Lee-Shannon when Jordan stopped him.

"Wait. What if they already know?" said Jordan. "What if that's the reason they want you to help James?"

Danion thought about it for a moment. It wasn't out of the realm of possibilities but if that was true why in the world they want James cursed?

"No." Danion said to her. "They wouldn't need James to come here to take the nexus they'll do it themselves."

"Are you sure?"

"It doesn't make any sense especially for what they have planned for… It wouldn't make any sense." he said before revealing too much about the Consortia's plans for James. "Helping a human steal Lore land they lose creditability across the entire spectrum. It just be easier for them to come here and take it themselves…and it's not something they haven't done before."

Jordan reluctantly had to agree with to that logic. She was still hesitant to trust the Consortia especially knowing that they wanted James to have the OC's land but she did trust Danion and he was right. Bringing in the Consortia would solve everything. She looked at him with his face saying 'Trust me'. It brought a comforting feeling over her as well as a smile that immediately vanished as a wave of splatter blood hit her in the face. Jordan blinded by the blood drops quickly wiped them away from her eyes only to see in horror a bloody arrowhead sticking out from Danion's chest. He looked down and slowly glided his finger across the wooden arrowhead sliding off a shred of pierced heart.

His heart.

He looked at it and gave a slight giggle then looked at Jordan with an expression as if he was never going to see the one he loved again.

"Rail..." he said falling to his knees and then the ground.

"No. No! NO!!" she yelled grabbing him and holding him in her arms so the arrow wouldn't go any deeper into his body. "Don't you leave me again! Please don't you leave me again!"

She held his face and looked into his eyes for signs of life.

"Look at me. Come on…look at me! You-are-not-dying!" Jordan ordered.

Danion looked up at Jordan seeing his focus on her getting very small with the space around her completely gone…but in that narrow point of view he did see something.

A red dot.

He watched as it moved its way up her body and steadying itself in position of Jordan's head. Danion tried to warn her but he could barely move or speak. Jordan too concerned about Danion didn't noticed the dot but for a split second her enhanced hearing caught the sound of something slitting the air towards her and before she could react a bullet…a sliver bullet entered the side of her head. Like a switch everything went black. Jordan fell back dropping Danion and making the arrow go deeper into his chest when his back hit the ground. The pain was intense but Danion pulled all his strength together to move himself to a position to see Jordan. There was blood all over the side of her face and a dead stare in her eyes. Danion tried to reach out to her only to see the skin on his hand turning chalky gray.

He was disintegrating

He knew he was going to die soon and with the last bit of strength grabbed hold of Jordan's bracelet tattooed wrist. Again, he tried to speak but it felt like dirt was choking his lungs. However, he was able to get two words out before everything faded to black.

"I do."

Yeah…it may sound a little corny, I know, but when you're seconds away from passing into the 'Great Beyond' it really doesn't matter if you're corny. But right now you're probably more concerned with what the hell just happened?

Hey…what's a good story without a surprise or two?

3

A Nexus.

Basically, it's a focal point where the mystical energies converge, some are famous like Stonehenge, The Bermuda Triangle, and Liberty Island. But most of them no one has ever heard of and that's the way the Consortia and other groups like 109 prefer it. You see a nexus can bend reality making the impossible possible ranging from time travel to crossing the dimension plain. Whoever controls a nexus and is capable of using its' power to become a very dangerous individual.
Yeah…yeah…you want me to skip the science lesson and get back to Danion and Jordan. Well that's the reason why I told you about a nexus. I'm sure that things that seemed 'unnatural' in the supernatural world are starting to make a little more sense now.

Well…some things.

With a gasp of air Jordan opened her eyes sitting up in a hotel room bed with a monstrous headache blazing through her skull screaming at the top of her lungs.

"It's alright! You're okay!" Kefflynn cried trying to relax her.

"Where am I?! I was shot!" Jordan cried with panting a breath and a jack-hammer heartbeat.

"No...the bullet grazed you. You're alright!" Keff promised.

"Alive? Alive." she said feeling her head and feeling a bandage.

Jordan started to smile as her senses awoke to the smell of someone's room service passing by the hotel room door and the sound of people and cars passing in the distance outside the hotel. They were simple things but a clear sign that she was really was alive...then her smile disappeared when she remembered what happened before she got shot.

"Danion..." she said with her heart sinking into her stomach. "Ohh...God no I can't go through this again. Not again! Please...not again."

"J...he's okay." said Keff.

"No...the arrow. I saw it go through his heart."

"It nicked his heart. It looked a lot worst than it really was."

"Where is he?" Jordan wanted to know.

"In the other room with your friend."

"What friend?"

"I don't know...some guy. 'Said he knew you two in Denver."

"Denver? That's impossible no one knew..." she paused possibly knowing who the 'friend' was. "Where's Danion?"

"In the other room." Keff said pointing to the connecting room doors.

Jordan got out of bed and staggered up to her feet. The pain in her head grew with each step but she was going into that other room.

"What are you doing? Don't try to walk. Get back into bed!" said Keff.

Keff tried flying in Jordan's path to stop her but Jordan was too big and too determined to be stopped, even as she use the wall to hold herself up. Jordan opened the connecting doors and saw Danion's hotel room in the Murdock with Danion laying on the bed inside. Though undead…he was still very alive.

She immediately rushed to him nearly falling twice. When she did get to him there was kissing, hugging, and other waves of emotion that Jordan didn't noticed that Danion was unconscious. She'd probably still been kissing him if she wasn't interrupted by an old friend.

And if you don't know 'who?'...I'm ending this story right now.

"What are you doing up?" I said.

Jordan looked over and saw me standing by the bathroom clearly stunned by my manly good looks but with her head still hurting she wasn't quick with an answer.

"I-I..."

"Well...that's not a reason." I told her.

I picked her up and started to carry her back to the other room but of course that wasn't going to happen.

"No." she said pointing back at Danion.

With the obvious choice of where she really wanted to be I took a deep breath and pulled a 180 back to Danion. I put her next to Danion and sat her up to check her out.

"Getting up after a head injury is not a good idea for humans or Lore." I said.

I reached into my pocket for a light-scope and started checking her eyes for any signs that her little walk did more harm than good. Not easy as she kept turning her head to look at the kid.

"Okay…I gonna ask you some questions. Answer them to the best of your abilities." I said. "What town is this?"

"Jackson Point?" she correctly answered.

"What's your name?"

"Jordan."

"Jord---? Oh…yeah you're using your middle name now."

"Who's she?" I asked her pointing at Keff.

"Kefflynn."

"Well…we're doing great so far. What day is this?"

"Uh…Tuesday?"

"Uhh…close enough." I said. "No need to ask you who the guy next to you is."

"Danion." she said turning to look at him again. "How---?"

"He'll be fine." I said. "His heart is already healing and that I.V. of blood is speeding up the process. He even opened his eyes a couple of times. Seemed real surprised to see me…probably thought he was in Hell...or San Bernardino…either 'who' he'll be up and about in no time."

"What are you doing here?" Jordan asked me.

"I'm on a pilgrimage to visit the better strip joints of the Canadian regions." I joked…sort of.

"I got a better question." said Keff. "Who are you?"

"Like I said over the phone…a friend."

Kefflynn looked over to Jordan for an answer.

"Sage." she told her.

"Yes…Sage." I repeated proudly to Keff. "And if you were five feet taller yours for a week.

Kefflynn again looked over to Jordan for an explanation. Jordan just shook her head in saying, 'Don't try'.

"Well…you don't look the worst for wear." I told Jordan. "But I want you to stay in bed, obviously it's gonna be this one, so get some sleep. Besides…I'm sure waking next to you will bring a speedy recovery to the kid."

I said that to get her to smile and it worked.

"All smiles aside." said Keff. "What the hell happened up there, J?"

"That can wait with other current events…right now it won't help her recovery." I told Keff who got the point along with Jordan unfortunately.

"What happened?" Jordan asked.

"Nothing." Keff lied.

"What happened?" Jordan demanded.

"Keff looked at me and I just put my hands up knowing who we were dealing with, So Keff told Jordan about the small group of trolls lead by the Major. It was quick and easy. They came in, took the Elder's Offspring, and got out leaving a note of James's demands to surrender the land. Also…that no OC or Gur-Fanng have the bright idea to come after James, making a very strong point that if they did the Offspring would never be seen again. That was nearly two days ago and attempts to find the Elder Offspring had failed making everyone believe with each passing moment that James had won. Keff couldn't believe that anyone would go to these extremes just to put up a building. That's when Jordan told us about her and Danion's discovery.

"A nexus? Here?" I said quickly becoming interested.

"We saw it." said Jordan. "It's there."

"Impossible. If the OC had a nexus I would know about it." said Keff.

"Danion thought you were probably keeping it a secret from the Gur-Fanng." said Jordan.

That didn't make Keff happy being accused of lying to her friends.

"Well...he's wrong." she told us.

"Maybe the Elders are keeping it from the rest of the OC." said Jordan.

"No. Wait." Keff paused. "Every once in a while…the Elders would go off to have a secret meeting. No one knows where they go but it was made pretty clear you weren't supposed to know."

"They could've been heading to the nexus." I said.

"Or probably playing poker which is a better theory." said Keff.

"Danion wanted to call the Consortia." said Jordan.

Keff and I looked at Jordan as if she was insane.

"Why?" Keff asked.

"The Consortia controls most of the nexuses." I said. "Probably the reason the Elders didn't tell anybody…they didn't want it taken away."

"He wanted to help." Jordan said taking Danion's hand.

"How?" said Keff not convinced.

"If the Consortia gets involved there's no way James could take your land." said Jordan. "But I stopped him."

"Why?" I asked.

"I wasn't sure that they didn't already know." she said

"What would make you think that?" I asked.

"Because..."

Jordan stopped herself...the news that Danion was working for the Consortia and that they wanted James to have the OC's land would not go well.

"...God, my head hurts." Jordan said to cover herself.

I could tell there was real pain there and the stress wasn't doing her any good either. So I told Jordan to rest and Keff to wake her every hour to make sure she really was sleeping and not in a coma. Head injuries tend to do that.

"Where are you going?" Keff asked me.

"Gonna find out if this nexus is the real deal." I answered grabbing my coat. "If it is it would explain a few things."

"How? You don't know where it is…besides since the Offspring were taken the OC and Gur-Fanng have been out in droves protecting the area. Right now anyone caught out there who's a stranger is not gonna get a warm welcome."

"Story of my life." I said.

Hours passed and Jordan rested comfortably next to Danion with her hand carefully resting on the bandages around his chest and heart. Every hour on the hour Keff woke up Jordan to see if she was still just sleeping. Each time feeling guilty because there was a look of peaceful pleasure in Jordan sleeping next to Danion and she kept disturbing it. At times Keff even caught a smile from Danion as if he knew Jordan was there.

It was a little after Keff's last check on Jordan that Danion opened his eyes. He felt her hand on his chest and scoped the area surprised to see that they were in his hotel room and…'alive?'.

At one point he wondered if they were both dead and this was a kind of heaven. Them together forever in the last place they made love was an idea he was quite agreeable with but the idea quickly passed as he felt a mass of pain in his chest as he sat up and wasn't there not supposed to be any pain in heaven. His movement woke Jordan and the two looked at each other with different expressions. Her… happy that he was finally awake. His…glad they were alive but perplexed as to how? So Jordan explained their massively good fortune but Danion wasn't convinced that anyone could be that excessively lucky.

"No. No…I've had my heart nicked by arrows I know the difference. That arrow went through my heart" he said.

"Then you'd be dead. You're not."

"There was a piece of my heart on the tip of the arrow…and I saw your head, there was so much...blood?" he said looking at the bandage that was now wrapped around her head and head-wound.

"I don't know what to tell you if you want to look a gift horse in the mouth…talk to Sage."

"Sage?" he said with widened eyes.

"Yeah…he's the one who patched us up."

Danion paused for a moment and thought about it…then nodded his head accepting things.

"Where's Sage now?" he asked.

"Checking out the supportive 'nexus' you say is out there." Keff said flying into the room. "I heard voices."

"It's there Keff." said Jordan.

"Says him."

"I saw it too."

Keff and Jordan looked at each other with a bit of friction. Not at each other but over Danion and where his loyalties may lay.

"Danion…this is Keff." said Jordan.
"Keff…Danion."

"We've met." Keff said with a harsh look towards Danion. "Craig can talk again now."

"About?" he asked.

Jordan turned to look at Keff…they both looked at her wondering if the secret of the two lovers was out.

"Nothing that would interest anybody." said Keff.

"Good." said Danion.

"You two should rest some more until your friend comes back." said Keff.

"No…I'm feeling better now. I'm just a little hungry." said Jordan.

"Then we'll order up some room service. You want anything?" Keff asked Danion.

"I'm covered." he said showing off his I.V. of blood.

Keff started to head to the phone next to the bed but Jordan discreetly put her hand over the phone and gave Keff the famous secret message of silence that only women can understand. This one saying, 'I want to be alone with my man'.

"I'll call from the other room." Keff said getting the message and disappearing into the other room.

"Hi." Jordan said looking at Danion with loving eyes.

"Hi."

"I'm glad you're not dead." she said.

"I'm glad you're not dead either." he said. "But be careful…that's how things got 'started' the last time we were here together."

"Oh…and we wouldn't want that to happen again." she said caressing the bandages over his chest.

"Ahgh…not a question of want but shouldn't." he said taking her hand away from his chest but yet still holding on to it.

"Danion we nearly died up there…for real this time."

"Yes…I know."

"Well we may not be so lucky next time. First time was a lie. Second…lousy shooting. Next time…?" she paused for a moment putting her hand that Danion was holding back on his chest.

"It just tells you when something comes along---Ah, fuck that! Are you gonna marry me or not?!"

"What?"

"You. Me. Married. Yes or no?"

Danion laughed at her directness

"Oh…this brings back memories." he said.

"Stop ducking the question. Yes or no?"

"Well. I don't know it's all so sudden." he said in a joking tone.

Jordan responded in typical fashion…hitting him in the chest.

"Owww!" he cried in pain.

"Sorry! Sorry!" she said trying to relieve the pain by rubbing his chest. "Are you okay?"

The pain was going away but the rubbing of his chest wasn't a good thing because it wasn't feeling really bad…if you know what I mean.

"I'm fine." he said. "I just... need a shirt."

"A shirt?"

"Yeah…there's one in the drawer." he said trying to get up with the I.V. line still in his arm.

"Stay here I'll get your shirt."

Jordan was feeling a lot better. She didn't feel as dizzy rising to her feet and walked with more stability when she went to open the drawer. She grabbed a shirt and that's when she saw it. Her eyes widened at the sight of it thinking it was gone forever, of course, she also thought the same of Danion. It simply didn't enter her mind, with Danion being alive and everything else that was going on, until she opened that drawer. The metal didn't shine the way it used to but that wasn't important. All that mattered, and I'm sure all you ladies can understand this, it was hers' again.

"What is it?" Danion asked.

The answer was immediate as Jordan turned around and Danion saw the bracelet he gave her 12 years ago.

"You kept it...all this time?" she said barely believing it.

"I had it sent to me after that night on the roof. 'Faster than overnight'. I don't even know why I did I just…did." he said.

"We both know why you did." she said walking back to him on the bed.

Danion didn't answer but he agreed with her. She climbed back into bed with him this time getting nose to nose with Danion. She looked into his eyes not saying a word but he knew what she wanted.

An answer.

He didn't know what to say. He clearly remembered saying 'I do' before the lights went out. He also knew that Jordan didn't hear it so in some way that was a good thing under the circumstances. But now Danion was up against the wall, confronted and not going anywhere with that I.V. in him he opted to do the unusual...tell the truth.

"I want to marry you." he said.

A huge smile appeared on Jordan's face only to quickly disappear after what Danion said next.

"But I can't. I honestly do want to marry you." he said surprising himself by his words. "But I can't…and before you ask 'Why?' I will tell you."

He explained…or at least tried to explain to her the complexities of things now. Not between him and her but just him alone. That he still had 'dealings' with the Consortia that had nothing do with James and couldn't…or wouldn't just 'take off' with her because of them. He was still hiding something, she knew it, but didn't know 'what?' or 'why?' and when she asked for details as expected he didn't give any. He just moved forward from the subject stating that the James situation wasn't over yet…and of course the new added mystery.

Who shot them both.

"I don't know." Jordan said drawing a blank for subjects.

"Neither do I and that's what worries me."

"Think the Consortia could have done it?"

"Why would you say that?"

"I've heard that they've killed their own for finding out things that they didn't want to be found out. Maybe they do know about the nexus." she said.

"It's not a nexus." I said coming through the connecting doors. "Hey kid…how's the chest?"

"Fine…and what do you mean it's not a nexus?" he asked.

"It's-not-a-nexus" I repeated more clearly. "I could see how easily you could think that but it's not. It's a Flex."

Okay…the difference between a nexus and a flex. A nexus is small about the size of a garage or house while a flex varies in sizes from an apartment to a mall parking lot. Nexuses are also stationary and consent. They're either on all the time or active on regular intervals. You know…once every forth-night or full moon. Flexes however tend to go active on their own whim and roam across a large area. Which explain the missing ships and planes in and over the Bermuda Triangle. I know…I just said the triangle was a nexus. The truth is it's both. You see…I tell you later it gets really complicated when you're sober. But the thing that truly separates a nexus from a flex is that a nexus is one thing. Either a reality bender, time twister, or dimension portal. A flex can be any, all, or more of these things at different or the same time.

Majorly cool…but something to be avoided whenever possible.

"Nexus or flex, James knows about it, and wants it." said Danion.

"Then he's a moron." I said. "No one has ever been able to control a flex. A nexus… sure 'cause its stable energy. But a flex is unpredictable. It's just a really bad thing to mess with."

"Then I better go with my original plan" said Danion.

"Calling the Consortia?" I asked.

Danion seeing that I knew about him and the Consortia immediately looked at Jordan.

"I told them you wanted to call the Consortia to tell them about the nex--- flex." she said expressing with her face that's all she told them.

"Good. I uh…still need to do that." said Danion.

"How?" I asked. "You don't find the Consortia…they find you."

"I got a way." he said.

"How and why would you have a way to find the Consortia?" I asked.

"Because I'm..."

Danion suddenly felt pressure on his arm from Jordan. When he looked at her Jordan's eyes were screaming 'Don't-Tell-Them!' but Danion could see in Keff's eyes she wanted an answer and wasn't going to settle for, 'I just do'.

"Because I'm working for them…undercover." he said.

"What?" Keff asked.

"Ahh, crap!" I cried.

"You're working for the Consortia?" cried Keff.

"'91?" I asked.

"Yeah...'91." he told me.

"'91?" asked Keff.

"It's a long story that no one wants to talk about. Let's move on." I told Keff.

"Fine…but why's he working undercover for the Consortia?"

The room got real quiet to Keff's question. Finally Danion spoke up giving a backstory about James, the Consortia, and himself. He said that James had been doing business with Lore for years. Nothing really new the Consortia monitors all big businesses that involve Lore. But James was always able to get the better part of the deal in every dealing with a variety of Lore. This was suspicious to the Consortia and since James had a strong will they couldn't just 'Jedi' him for an answer. So they came up with another option…a mole. Danion was a bit fuzzy on how he got into James's employ but he got in none the less and for the last two years worked to make sure that James's more 'unique deals' with Lore and humans went through with no complications, all the while keeping taps on James for the Consortia.

"So, you're the one who hired the mercs?" asked Keff.

"They were already recruited by the time I got here." said Danion.

"And who's idea was it to use trolls to attack the OC village?" Keff asked clearly knowing what the answer was but just wanting to hear it.

"Mine." he said not denying it.

"And was it your idea to kidnap the Elder Offspring?" asked Kefflynn

Jordan looked at Danion. She knew the answer remembering what he said to her on her apartment roof.

Again…he didn't deny it.

"Yes." he said.

"You sonvabitch!" Keff yelled with a flying charge that I stopped by grabbing the ends of her feet.

"And what are you going to do little fairie?" I asked her. "In this corner…vampire. In the other…fairie. 'Like a white guy against Tyson."

"He's the reason the Offspring got napped." said Keff.

"And he's probably the reason you'll get them back." I said looking at Danion. "Fantastic plan being worked out...I hope."

"The Consortia. Get them here and everything will be fine." he said.

"Well...how do we do that?" asked Jordan.

"It's not as hard as you think..." I said opening my big fat mouth but lucky a sudden revelation by Kefflynn saved me from explaining myself.

"Waitaminute... if you're working for the Consortia then they know James is after our land." she said.

I could see that Danion knew where this was going and that was not a good thing.

"But you've been helping James try to get the land...and they would know about that too"

The expression on Jordan's face was not a good one as she worried about Keff piecing it all together.

"If they knew that... then why wouldn't they try to stopped James. Unless..."

"I would think before you finish that thought." stressed Danion.

"Oberon..." Keff said seeing that what she was thinking was now confirmed.

"Keff..."

"You knew." she looked at Jordan. "That's why you thought the Consortia knew about the flex. You knew that they were helping James!"

"They're not helping James...completely." said Danion.

"What's that's supposed to mean?" Keff asked.

"It means the questions you don't ask keeps you breathing." I told Keff. "But about getting word to the Consortia?"

"There's a way." said Danion.

"How?" Jordan asked.

Danion's eyes moved over to Keff as the answer.

"You have to go to the Elders." he told her.

"And do what?" Keff asked perplexed on what she could do.

"Tell them to tell 'her' about the flex." he said.

"Tell who?" asked Keff.

"Doesn't matter." said Danion. "If they want their land back and James out of their collective asses tell them to tell 'her' about the flex.

"And their gonna know what this means?"

"Yes." He said to Keff.

Danion didn't say anymore. It was clear to everybody he was not going to say anymore.

"Okay…liking the plan but let's modify it a bit by letting Keff put your little message in the written word instead of in person." I said. "That way no one…meaning the Consortia…can figure out we know about them. Making everybody a whole lot safer…more importantly *me* a whole lot safer. Well…I'm stressed I'm gonna go hit the Internet."

"What for?" Asked Danion.

"To download porn to relax me." as if the answer wasn't obvious. "Keff…you've got a letter to deliver. You two stay in bed and rest… and I mean 'rest'. Also…pray to whoever gods you believe in that all of this works out and none of us gets killed. Really liking that last part to happen."

"I'm gonna go but I'll be back…and we're gonna talk about a few things." Keff said to Jordan then looking at Danion with a very unhidden sense of hostility.

I quickly ushered Keff through the connecting doors and closed them behind me leaving our two lovers alone.

"Your friend doesn't like me." said Danion.

"Can you blame her?" said Jordan. "You just admitted that it was your idea to destroy her home village, and kidnap OC to help James…why?"

"'Cause it's the truth and I've done worse in other places. Things that will follow me for a very long time…and probably anyone else who's involved with me." he said to her.

She was getting his hidden message and responded to it.

"So…you've done shit since Denver." she said. "Hello…so have I. It keeps me up nights like your shit keeps you up days but you wanna know what…I don't constantly dwell on it to make my life a living hell or scare people away. Alright…admittedly there are things and people you don't get over but there are other things you just need to get over. So, when all this is over you and me are going to find a quiet spot...tell each other the shit we've done…then get over it and move on."

"To what?" he asked sensing the meaning in 'move on'.

"Well…that's up to you, isn't it?" You wanna marry me but you won't." she said.

You could tell by her tone she wasn't happy. She knew that Danion's barriers of mysteries and secrets were just a way from giving a clear and precise 'Yes' or 'No'.

"Listen I---"

"Don't." she said cutting him off. "I don't wanna hear it again or some new version of it. So please…don't."

She laid back on the bed her back subjectively turned to him. The next hour was very quiet but as it passed the two started unconsciously or maybe even instinctively moving slowly from opposite sides of the bed to the center of it.

No guesses to what happened next.

No words were spoken. It's started with a look…then a kiss…and went on from there. It was nothing too physical since they were still recovering but they clearly expressed to each other how they were both glad the other was alive.

The sun was starting to come up over Jackson Point and Danion and Jordan were up and about. The bandages around her head were now just one bandage on the side of her head. Danion's I.V. got him back on his feet, also a night with Jordan helped. There was still some pain around the chest but the kid was riding through it pretty well.

I had some news to give and I felt it would be better to tell them in my trusty 'ole winnebago who I affectionately called Carla. She was work of art. A 197--- well, she doesn't like me telling her age. Okay so she was a little beat up in some areas, her tires a little bald and there was a cracked window...or two. But you had to love the large Lime-green strip that wrapped around her and the fact she always got me from point 'A' to point 'B'. Yep, Carla was one of the few females who stayed with me for an extended period of time, and that's what made her beautiful to me.

Jordan on the other hand had quite a different opinion of Carla.

"You actually drive around in this piece of junk?" she asked looking at Carla with distaste

"Hey…do not insult my girl." I said opening up Carla's side door. "Besides…like everything else it isn't the outside that matters but the inside."

"Sage, I use to live in a trailer park and I still wouldn't live in... this?"

I love seeing the jaws drops of new people who see Carla's interior that has an uncanny resemblance to one of those spacious high ceiling New York warehouse apartments that cost $3.500 a month. Immediately Jordan jumped outside and checked out the dimensions of Carla's exteriors and saw that Carla's outside would easily fit in her inside.

"It's amazing what you can do when you combine Popular Mechanics and some home improvement videos from YouTube." I said to Jordan as she came back in still not believing what she was seeing.

"Magic." she said looking at Danion who she noticed wasn't surprised by Carla.

"You've redecorated." he said.

"A new coat of paint does wonders." I said. "But right now I really want to talk to you about calling in the Consortia. Not saying it's not a good plan but there's no guarantee that the Elders are gonna get their kids back. More than likely the Consortia will be more concerned about getting the flex then helping the OC."

"That's cross my mind." said Danion.

"And...?"

"And...I can just go back to James to find where the Elder Offspring are and get them back."

"Not highly recommended since James is probably the one who shot you both."

There was a dramatic pause there.

"James shot us?" Danion said with a voice of disbelief and subtle anger.

"Well…it's either him or the Consortia and since the Consortia is really good at making people stay dead, I'm going with James." I said.

"Why?" Jordan asked.

"My guess…he probably thought Danion here was betraying him to the OC and the Gur-Fanng."

"How do you figure that?" Danion asked me.

Well…I told them that after my little…'stress relief' with the Internet I focused back on a few questions involving Danion and Jordan but I wasn't really getting anywhere, so I hit the couch…watched a repeat of the original MacGyver and drunk myself into a root-beer float coma. However, as I miraculously regain consciousness everything became so abundantly clear. You'd be surprised by how simple things become when you black out.

"Somewhere down the line James got suspicious of you and probably had you followed---"

"I was never followed." Danion said. "I would know if I was."

"Really? Sure you haven't been kinda...distracted lately?" I asked glancing over to Jordan.

Danion reluctantly agreed with silence.

"How can you be sure on this?" he then asked.

I smiled at them like a 10-year-old who had a big secret that no one else knew. Yeah...it was childish but it was a chance to shine and I don't get too many opportunities to show that I can do more than walk and chew gum at the same time. So, I showed them the first clue, which was the arrow that went through Danion.

"Noticed anything interesting?" I said tossing the arrow to him.

It took him a second but he finally figured out.

"It's a crossbow arrow." he said.

"And elves don't use crossbows. An elf can fire 10 arrows from a regular bow by the time you reload a crossbow. They also don't use guns. Well...most of them don't." I said looking at Jordan.

"Okay...James shoots me to keep me from helping the OC and the Gur-Fanng but why take out Jordan?" Danion asked.

"Well...if you were followed you definitely would have been seen together. Maybe Jordan got shot because he was afraid she knew too much."

"Maybe? You're not sounding too sure about that?" said Jordan.

"Truth be told..." I reluctantly started. "It doesn't make sense to kill either one of you." The smart thing to do is to keep you alive to feed you false information or find out how much the OC and Gur-Fanng knew first. Maybe James panicked. I don't know."

"James doesn't panic." said Danion.

"Maybe he would if he really thought I knew too much." said Jordan.

Both intrigued by that statement Danion and I looked at her to explain it.

"James wants the land for the flex, right?"

"Right." said Danion.

"The O.C....or at least the Elders know about the flex. Since the Gur-Fanng are their allies he might think that---"

"The Gur-Fanng would know about it, too." Danion said finishing her sentence. "It makes sense. James tried to kill us because---"

"Because he was afraid I would tell you about the flex." she said finishing his sentence.

"Whoever shot us probably did it thinking you were showing me the flex never knowing we just stumbled across it." said Danion.

"Killed you to keep you from knowing. Kill me from telling you." said Jordan.

"Kids...I hate to disagree with two people who could obviously kick my ass but that doesn't make sense either." I said. "Why kill Danion for knowing about the flex? I mean there's no reason behind it unless he knew you were working for the Consortia and was afraid you were gonna...tell them."

The room got quickly quiet by my little statement.

"If James knew you were working for the Consortia..."

"He would want me dead before I could tell them about the flex." Danion said again finishing Jordan's sentence.

"How long could he have known?" I asked.

"At the least...the few days I've been here." said Danion. "At the most...two years."

"How could he have found out?" asked Jordan.

"I don't know but it explains why I was never told about the flex in the first place." said Danion. "But there's no way he could have known I was working for the Consortia unless he could smell them on me."

Danion's eyes suddenly widened in silence. Jordan and I both could see that something made him believe his last statement was a possibility and a not small joke…and from the look on his face this was not a good thing.

"What?" Jordan asked.

"Nothing." he said.

Jordan had heard the tone in his 'nothings' before to know it was something.

"What?" she repeated this time grabbing him by the coat collar to get an answer.

His mind race…should he tell her or shouldn't he tell her. Right now she knew more than she was supposed to know so why not tell her more.

"The Consortia wanted me to spy on James to find out his secrets with dealing with Lore. Maybe the secret is he is… Lore." he said with hesitation.

"James is Lore?" Jordan said stunned by the news.

"No…it can't be. In the two years I been working for James there was never a sign that he even might be."

"He can't be…Lore always know each other." she said.

"Actually…there are some Lore can mask themselves from others." I said.

"Who?" asked Jordan.

"High level demons….Drac-cul…some shape-shifters."

"Drac-cul?" Danion said with interest in hearing the name of the top vampire caste.

"Yeah" I answered. "That's why they're so rarely ever seen. You can't sense or smell them out like the other vampir---Whoa...! You don't think James is a Drac-cul?"

"I had to pay those trolls in gold. Gold coins to attack the OC village. When that went south I had to pay them more for the second plan. I wasn't surprised that James could get the money but I did wonder how he could get that much in gold coins that fast." Said Danion "Legends says that Drac-cul have vaults of hoarded treasure from the centuries."

"You're basing James is a Lore on that?" I said.

"Looking at things a little differently there have been other things since my first day with James but still it all could be a 'maybe'."

"If James was a Drac-cul could he have known you were with the Consortia." said Jordan.

"How?" he asked.

"I don't know Smelled them on you…sense them somehow. The say Drac-cul are psychic." she said.

"That's a myth that they have perpetrated, but if you lied about your whereabouts or who you were meeting that's when he could've been found out." I said.

It was all starting to come together. If James was a Lore and somehow found out that Danion was working for the Consortia there was no way he could tell Danion about the flex in fear that they would take it from him. Going on that if James thought Jordan was going to show Danion the flex he had to take the kid out before he could get word back to the Consortia.

"Waitaminute this only pans out if James is a Lore and I'm telling you I don't know for sure." said Danion.

"Then let me hit the net again…do some background on James and see if I can get a hit." I said.

"What could you find that the Consortia couldn't?" asked Danion.

I looked at him with an insulted expression and answered accordingly.

"Rule#1 in the 'Book of Sage'. We never doubt his skills. His courage…sure. His masculinity…okay…and maybe that one time in West Hollywood his sexual identity but never his skill to uncover information." I said.

I headed back to my computer and started to get to work with Danion looking over my shoulder like an 8th grade science teacher. His frustration was clearly showing the first twenty minutes in believing that no progress was being made, I however saw a lot of things that raised an eyebrow. I was about to let Danion in on those things when I saw him staring at Jordan who was exploring the wide spaces of Carla. I've seen that look in the eyes of many a person…the one that says that I'm in love with that person. Unfortunately, with the joy of love I could see a sadness that was going to keep that love from happening. I've seen that look just as many times...my own face included.

"Marry her." I told him. "She may not ask again."

Danion looked at me with the 'How do you know?' expression. Easy…Keff and I were listening through the door before I told them about the flex.

"And...?" he asked, I guessed wanting to hear my two cents on things.

"And Keff thinks you're not good enough for J."

"She's probably right." said Danion

"Phooey. Take it from somebody who hasn't had many opportunities in love. So he's filled the void with cheap sex with a multitude of women…sometimes with a multitude of women at the same time." I said pausing to recall a certain memory.

"Your point?" Danion asked.

"What?... Oh yeah. Marry her…you want to." I said.

"It's complicated." he said.

"How complicated?" I asked.

"None of your business complicated." he stated.

"Well..." I said getting the point. "If there is a wedding let's hope it fares better than the first time you two saw each other again. Heard it wasn't the most romantic of reunions."

"Oh yeah." Danion said recalling that not-so-fond memory. "First…she sinks her teeth into my shoulder and tries to stake me. Then after that tries to rip my arm off."

"She bit you?" I asked.

"Twice."

"Did you uh...bite her back?"

Danion probably thought I asked the question in the sense of a 7-year-old saying, 'He hit me, I hit him back.' but I was very interested in the answer.

"'Had to get her off me." he said.

And right then things started to make sense for me about Danion and Jordan getting shot. Not who shot them but how they survived.

How they really survived.

Oh…come on people you didn't really buy that crap I told Keff, did you? That only happens in comic books and bad soap operas.

I instantly started pacing the room in a feverish rate. I couldn't believe what I was thinking but it was adding up. It made sense even though it was impossible.

"It can't be. Could be." I mumbled to myself. "She bites him. He bites her. Add the flex…it could happen."

"What's going on?" Jordan asked Danion.

"He's...being Sage." he answered.

"That has to be it. Has to be. Damn." I excitedly said.

"Sage! What is it?" Danion asked cautious for my answer.

I opened up the drawer and pulled out a spent bullet…a silver bullet and tossed it over to Jordan.

"That's the bullet I pulled outta your head." I told her.

She looked at the bullet with dried blood on it and then at me with obvious confusion.

"But you told Keff---"

"Oh...that's easy to explain…I lied." I said. "There was a bullet in your skull and an arrow through your heart. Didn't either of you question how you could have survived something like that?"

"Wasn't that you?" said Danion.

I stared at him with a raised eyebrow on that statement.

"What do you mean by that?" I asked very interested in the answer.

"Nothing...just that you patched us up after you found us...right?" he said.

"How did you find us anyway?" Jordan asked.

"Don't change the subject now that were on the verge of a major Lore event." I said heading to the frig.

"That being?" asked Danion.

"The dawn of the new Lore...the Vam-wolf." I announced tossing a couple of pieces of fruit to them.

There was a moment of silence as the two looked at me and then at each other to the news.

It was Danion who started laughing first.

"Are you actually trying to tell me the reason we are alive is because we're---"

"Vam-wolves!" I said finishing his sentence.

Danion laughed again, Jordan with him this time.

"Alright it's a little crazy to take---"

"Try impossible." said Jordan. "Werewolves and vampires have been fighting and biting each other for...ever. Why are we so suddenly special?"

"Because of the flex." I told them. "You two could have easily been exposed to it up there without knowing it."

Remember…a flex has the power to bend physical reality making things possible where they weren't before. Jordan was right, vampire and werewolves have always been immune to each other bites but that may have not been the case within the flex allowing the blending of two ancient enemies to become one with the other.

Jordan wasn't laughing so much after that explanation.

"Could that be possible?" she looked at Danion.

"Of course not." Danion said.

"Really? That is a silver bullet that was inside her head. She should be dead right now. Regardless of that little fact I've seen werewolves shot in the head with regular bullets. It takes weeks if not months to regenerate the gray matter to form a two-word sentence let alone the walkin' and talkin' you're doing." I told Jordan. "Very few Lore have the ability to grow back brain-cells that fast. One of them is a vampire."

Then it was Danion's turn.

"And you…you should be dust right now" I said to him. "No vampire expect a Drac-cul has ever survived a direct piecing of the heart. You're alive...so to speak because a werewolf can survive a stake through the heart."

I could see that Jordan was at least open to the possibility that maybe it could happen but in Danion's face I saw a flat out 'No'.

"Finally...and I think this is a major point on things for the last three minutes... Danion's been eating."

Danion and Jordan didn't notice that in the time I was speaking Danion nearly finished off the apple I tossed him.

Vampires don't eat.

They stared at it like it was the forbidden fruit...always there yet never attainable. The apple fell from Danion's hand as he looked at Jordan with some chewed apple still in his mouth that he quickly swallowed.

"Man...do you know what this could mean?" I said to them. "A werewolf immune to silver. A vampire who can survive being staked. Holy water. Sunlight! That could be just the beginning. Who knows how far this could go. Oh...I gotta start writing this stuff down."

"What you should be doing is getting all you can on James." said Danion.

"James? Screw James this could be bigger than the Gray." I said.

"What's the Gray?" Jordan asked.

"Please...don't get him started on that one." begged Danion. "James still has the Elder Offspring as a bargaining chip and I can tell you the Consortia would easily sacrifice them for the flex."

With that motivation I went back to my computer console and pulled up all the information I had on James. I told them from the very beginning that things seemed off with James. When Danion asked 'How so?' I showed an article about James on the screen. The headline read '15-year-old becomes millionaire.', explaining how James made his millions through the stock market yet there was no picture of a young James with the article. You would think that a kid making more money in a day then most do their entire lives would earn a picture. Then again, the story didn't have sex, murder, or a high pubic official, so why waste the film. But what struck me curious was what he did with the money after he made it. Not what he bought but what he didn't buy.

"A car?" Danion asked looking at me thinking the reason was stupid. "You think James is a Lore because he didn't buy a car."

"No…he bought a car to be chauffeured around but he never bought himself a sport car after his 16th birthday. Sixteen, a millionaire, and you don't buy yourself Lamborghini, Ferrari, or corvette? I don't think so." I said. "No 16-year-old---No 16-year-old male would do that…they're getting a car."

"Why?" Danion asked.

Jordan and I told him with the most obvious answer…

"To get laid."

I continued to tell them that James was emancipated shortly after he made his millions. I did a background on his parents. Father…unknown. Mother…dead. Not just dead also cremated. Now that happened before James got rich so how was he able to play the market as a minor…remember this was pre-internet days. Also, James's education is something of a question mark. Yeah…I admit some people are just naturally gifted like myself but James seemed to be self-educated with a variety of tutors, yet I was not able to find any of them, or any evidence that they were paid. Any schools before that I couldn't find. Now there are two possibilities on that…the school or schools closed down…or James changed his name from something else and that's why I could barely find anything, which could also explain why he doesn't have much of a social life. I checked phone records and other than business acquaintances James had no long term or continuous calls to or from anyone.

Not a one.

"So James doesn't have any friends because he's an asshole…big deal." said Jordan.

"It's unnatural for a person to have a past that's more paper and software than living testimonials like friends and family." I said.

"His past is not really consistent. One reason why anyone might think he is Lore." said Danion.

"Well I wouldn't blame them the only people who have past like this are in Witness Protection or Lore hiding in the human mainstream. Since protected witnesses tend to keep a low profile the old paranoid-meter is screaming 'Lore'" I said.

"Lore or human James still has to be dealt with." said Danion.

"Especially about trying to kill us." said Jordan in a seemingly 'Breaker' tone.

"Don't think human or Lore is gonna survive that." I said.

"You think James really is a Lore?" Jordan asked me.

"It's a maybe…possible." I said.

I brought up another article about James on the computer screen. This one had a picture of James's at his big debut to the business world as he was beginning international company 15 years ago…then I showed Jordan a picture of James at stock-holders dinner last year.

"Either he keeps himself in very good shape or has a very good plastic surgeon but there's no denying it he's very well preserved." I said showing that in 15 years James hadn't seemed to age.

Suddenly Jordan started staring at me. Something I really don't mind from a pretty lady but her stare was more examination than attraction.

"What?" I asked.

"Nothing...it's just that it's been about 12 years and you haven't seemed to age much either...or at all."

"Well…I have a very good plastic surgeon." I smiled with a wink.

She then looked over to Danion who was pacing the room. What was he thinking I do not know but Jordan saw a chance to re-open a subject.

"You don't really think this Vam-wolf thing is real, right?" she asked me.

"'Explains how you two survived the other night." I repeated. "And how you broke that troll's fingers. Werewolves are strong but not as strong as 10-foot trolls. Your strength probably double---Hell, tripled since the kid's a House.

"So…what's the flip-side?" she asked.

"Meaning?"

"Meaning sunlight doesn't kill werewolves but what would it do to a Vam-wolf?"

"Why would you ask?"

"I've... noticed that the sun seems really 'bright' lately…and 'hot' like a Denver summer." she said. "I didn't put much thought into it till you brought up the Vam-wolf thing."

"Okay..." I said seeing some concern in her face. "First thing…you don't panic. Just avoid direct sunlight for a while till we can get some tests done."

"He'll never go for that." Jordan said motioning her eyes over to Danion about him taking tests, knowing that he still didn't put any stock in my Vam-wolf theory.

"You'll convince him" I said. "Hell…you'll have it down to a fine science by the time you get hitched."

"How did you know---?"

"How is not the question it's when." I said. "As in when is the big day?"

"Never if it's up to him." she said.

"Then don't leave it be up to him."

She looked at me like I had an answer when she was the answer.

"Little advice…men are morons." I told her. "And sometimes you just have to tell them what's good for them."

She thought about it then nodded her head in understanding.

She got up and started to walk to Danion to tell him what the skinny was when Kefflynn started banging outside on Carla's door. I opened the door and she flew in heading straight for Jordan.

"Keff…you delivered the letter already?" she asked.

Keff explained she didn't even get a chance to write it. As soon as she got home there was a message from another fairie telling her what had recently happened at the OC village. A box was dropped in front of the village and brought to the Elders. Inside was a note that read, 'Your land or your children.' A clear and direct threat to the future existence of the Elder Offspring. A threat that was taken very seriously by what else was in the box...a pair of torn off fairie wings.

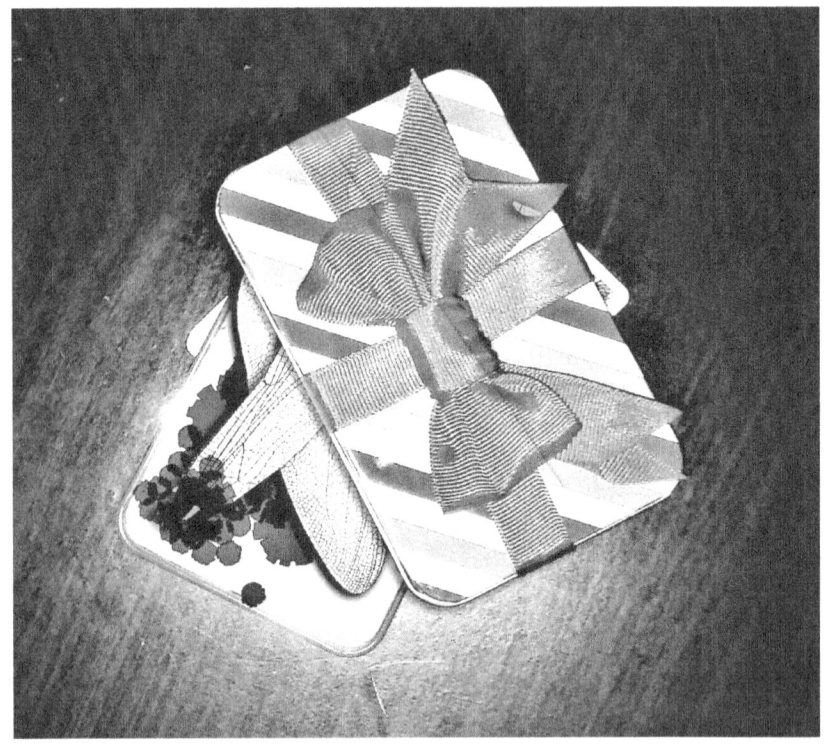

"We've lost." said Keff. "They're giving up. They're not risking the Offspring."

"So...it's over?" Jordan asked in disbelief.

"It's not over...James cannot be allowed to control that flex." said Danion.

"And how do you plan on stopping him? The Consortia? Well they've been doing a bang-up job helping us so far." Keff said darting her eyes at Danion for his part against the OC.

"We need to stick with the plan and get the Elders to call the Consortia. " said Danion.

"What good would that do now?" asked Keff.

"James won't get the land." answered Danion.

"What good does that do for the Offspring…remember what you said earlier." I reminded Danion.

"What I said earlier has a simple solution." he said. "We find the Offspring and we bring them back. More to the point James is going to tell me where they are and I'll bring them back."

"You really think he's gonna tell you anything?" asked Keff.

"Once I start removing his internal organs, yes…I think he'll tell me a lot." said Danion.

"Whoa…Dr. Kill-Everybody." I said. "The Lore issue on James hasn't been confirmed or denied yet."

"What issue?" Keff asked.

"James might be a Lore." said Jordan.

"James is a Lore?" Keff said clearly stunned by the news. "What kind?"

"We don't know yet. Could be a Drac-cul…and if that's true your little encounter will end really quickly…and not in your favor." I said.

"We don't have time to deal with what might be but to focus on what is." said Danion. "James has the Elder Offspring. The OC will surrender their land by this time tomorrow and James will have control of the flex. Now…getting the Consortia involved will stop James but 3 to 1…they'll care more about getting the flex than saving the Offspring. So it's up to us to get them back."

All of us knew that Danion was right but he was missing a few key facts, and at the risk of my stunningly good looks, I had to tell him. James tried to kill him. Worst case scenario was that James knew that Danion was working for the Consortia and decided to take him out before he could inform them about the flex. Now going on that theory, showing up to beat the crap out of James when he thinks Danion is dead is not a good idea, James would assume that the Consortia knows about the flex. No way James can take on the Consortia so maybe he'll have cut his losses and get the hell out of Dodge, or maybe…just maybe in a feat of rage over losing the flex he decides to kill the Offspring out of spite. A big possibility after those torn fairie wings.

Danion thought about it and had to consider that it could happen. So he asked if anyone had any better ideas. Keff came up with one. The OC surrenders the land, gets the Offspring back, then calls the Consortia to get the land away from James. One problem...once the Consortia had the land would they allow the OC to live on it again? Keff suggested that they be more willing if the Lore suddenly found out that the Consortia was helping a human steal Lore land. We told her that idea would probably get us all killed.

"Any other ideas?" I asked.

"Bottom-line...we need to get the Offspring away from James without him knowing you're involved." Jordan said to Danion. "Then we can deal with him anyway we want."

"And how do we do that without confronting James...he's probably the only one who knows where they are." I said.

"What about the one who kidnapped them, the...Major? He would know, right?" asked Jordan.

"He's probably held up safe guarding them." said Danion. "No way James is going to leave that job alone to trolls."

"Well...is there anyone else?" Jordan asked.

Danion shook his head for an answer and was about to say 'NO' when a possibility popped inside his head that gave a little hope to the situation.

"Wait...there might be someone." he said.

"Who?" I asked.

"Davis. James's accountant/ footstool. He might know where the Offspring are." said Danion.

"Think you can get anything out of him?" asked Jordan.

"He's not that strong willed. James tells him to 'Shut-up', he shuts-up." said Danion. "If I can get him alone...get the info…then wipe his memory clean, James won't be the wiser."

"But does he know anything?" I asked.

This guy follows James like a lap-dog. In fact…in the two years I was working for James I don't think I've ever seen Davis more than thirty feet away from him. He has to know where the Offspring are and... probably everything else." it suddenly occurred to him. "I could find out if James really knows about the flex."

"A Daisy." I thought out load.

"What?" Jordan asked.

"A Daisy. Davis could be James's daywatcher." I said. "It's the unofficial nickname for a vampire lapdog. Like in the movies the little guy who eats bugs and takes Dracula's crap and loves every minute of it."

"Sage, not now." Danion said.

"Listen…if this guy is a daywatcher this may not be as easy as you think. They're extremely loyal to their masters. You may not be able to get anything out of him." I said.

"'Guess I'll find out tonight." Said Danion.

"Tonight?" I asked knowing and not liking the answer. "Kid…not a good idea."

"Well…I'm running out of options." he said.

"Well…look harder!" I shouted.

They all looked at me with shocked expressions. I apologized I usually don't have outbursts like that but I don't have many friends in the long-term sense and I hate to lose one just because he didn't have the common sense to listen to me.

Unfortunately with the 'James being a Lore' still a question mark and time running out the kid was determined to go and find out anything he could from Davis to get the Offspring back. Not really surprising…Danion always had this thing when he knowingly or unknowingly did something wrong he would do whatever it took to make it right. Of course, that changed in the past few years but now something…or someone had him back on the old path.

So…knowing that I appealed to Jordan.

"If you have any influence over him I suggest you use it now." I told her. "If James is a Lore--- If he's a Drac-cul, you do not want Danion taking the chance of running into him…especially at night."

"I know." said Jordan. "That's why I'm going with him."

Completely forgot who I was talking to when it came to determination…aka outright stubbornness. Danion and Jordan were two of a kind and after the Quinns in Brotherhood 12 years earlier I knew I didn't have a chance of talking either one out of what they were planning. So right there I started praying to whatever gods were listening because if things decided to go bad, Danion and Jordan could actually end up really dead this time.

And if you've been following this story from the beginning you know things were going to go bad.

It was close to 5:00 in the AM when Danion and Jordan arrived at James's house. It took a lot of convincing to get them to wait all night so Danion could make his move on Davis but if James was a Drac-cul and something went wrong, facing him closer to sunrise would be a whole lot better than sunset.

"So…you ready?" Jordan asked.

"Yeah…stay here and I'll be back." he said.

"I'm going with you."

"No you're not."

"You need a look out."

"No I don't."

"If Sage is right---"

"If Sage is right I don't want you anywhere near that place." he said.

"If Sage is right I'm definitely going." she said. "You are not going to get yourself killed before I….Listen I'm not gettin' in a fucking argument with you. I am going in there with you, period…and before you say anything…one hour…the sun…let's go."

Getting into the house was no problem and once inside they headed to Davis's bedroom on the first floor. Jordan waited outside as the look-out as

Danion went inside to get the information out of Davis.

Davis's eyes opened in a panic as he felt a hand covering his mouth. When he looked up and saw Danion the looked in his eyes turned to shock.

"Say 'Hello'." Danion said lifting his hand from Davis's mouth.

"Hello." he said as Danion pulled him out of bed to his feet.

"From the look on your face you seemed very surprised to see me alive." said Danion.

Davis stared at him and nodding his head, 'Yes'.

"One question answered…now here is another…Did James tried to kill us?"

Davis nodded again.

"Because I found out about the flex?"

"Flex? I thought it was---I don't know what you're talking about." lied Davis.

Danion slightly slammed Davis against the wall to get a better answer.

"Yes...Yes he did." Davis said quickly changing his story. "Does the Consortia know? The mas--- Mr.

James will be very upset if the Consortia knew about the nexus...or flex"

"Another question answered...he did know I was spying for the Consortia." said Danion. "Well. Your mas--- Sorry, Mr. James is going to be very, very, upset."

"Then they do know?" Davis said with a near paniced tone.

"They will." said Danion. "Now...where are the Elder Offspring?"

"I can't tell you that."

Another knock against the wall by Danion happened.

"I won't tell you that." said Davis.

"Yes, you will." Danion said looking into Davis's eyes to hypnotize him.

"No...I won't."

Suddenly Danion felt a rush of pain as Davis started crushing his wrist. Danion looked at him this time with a shocked look on his face as he couldn't break Davis's hold.

"You see Danion I'm sure you can understand..." Davis said while forcing Danion down to one knee. "That I won't be telling you or anybody else where the Elder Offspring are until I get my land, and more importantly my nex--- I apologize and correct myself. My flex!"

Jordan turned to Davis's door when she heard the raised voice inside. Before she could react Danion came crashing through the door with such a force that he went flying through the wall across the hall. Jordan rushed to Danion who was unconscious on the floor. As she was checking him she felt a present behind her. It was Davis sporting a friendly smile towards her and she could clearly tell there was a sinister emotion behind that smile.

"So…you're alive as well." he said. "I really must get better help than what I already have."

"Oh my god." Jordan said looking at Davis with disbelief.

"I really don't think he's going to help you right now." said Davis.

Immediately Jordan went into full werewolf mode and charged at Davis, claws out in an effort to protect Danion. With one swipe of a claw Davis was gone only to reappear behind her.

"Here it is." he said in a relaxed tone. "Your skills are truly wasted on me. So why even try."

Unfortunately she did try and like Davis said it was a wasted effort. Like a child fighting a fully-grown adult it was no contest. He dodged her claws as if they were coming at him in slow motion. He even did a comic book movie move of blocking the Jordan's claws with one hand to amuse himself. Finally he just got bored and disappeared right in front of her. She looked around and saw a heavy mist starting to surround her.

It seemed to be whispering and coming at her at all sides until a force inside the mist knocked her against the wall so hard that it left an impression. She fell to the floor unconscious next to Danion reverting back into human form. Davis also returned to human form from the mist and stood over Danion and Jordan shaking his head in a 'I told you so' matter.

"Young Lore." he said. "Think they can take on the world."

The Drac-cul.

So much to tell and so little time to tell it. Long ago I said they were not just the top of the line of vampires but were above it. Where there are thousands of House and thousands of Brood, there were less than 200 Drac-cul across the world. They are extreme if not fanatical about whom the bring into their ranks. It's said that ten Drac-cul have to agree before one can bring someone across. Their connection to Dracula has always been a subject of multi-layers from Dracula being the first Drac-cul, to the novel being based on one in their caste. Whatever the truth or fiction that surrounds those theories and the many more that worked in the Drac-cul's favor giving them a mystique that's overshadowed the majority of Lore legends. Their powers are a long list between super-enhanced strength and transmutation but the one thing that has put them above all other vampires is their ability to walk in the sun.

Davis watched as the sunlight shined through the sliding glass doors of the back of his house. With a sip of coffee he enjoyed the view of the landscape and got closer to the glass to feel the heat of the rays without the chilled exposure of a Canadian morning. A good sight to start the day with but it was quickly interrupted by the stirring moans of Danion tied to a chair.

"Ah…you're awake. I was beginning to think you were going to be out all day." said Davis.

Danion tried to move but the ropes were too thick to break in a sudden burst then his eyes caught something lying next to him.

"J-Jordan." he called out to her seeing that her arms and legs were wrapped in chains.

No response.

"What have you done to her?" asked Danion.

"Nothing permanent." said Davis. "Would you like some coffee? It's from Italy. It's quite good. A little blood makes it even better."

"I want to know what you've done to her." Danion repeated.

"We fought…she lost." Davis replied. "I used chains for her since her claws could probably cut through those ropes, but don't worry, she's fine…in fact she woke up sometime before you did, she just pretending to be unconscious to fool me. Isn't that right, Ms.?"

They both looked at Jordan who was silent and not moving.

"Isn't that right, Ms.?" Davis repeated encouraging Jordan to answer.

She didn't.

"Very well…perhaps if I take your boyfriend outside in the sun you'll be a tad more cooperative." said Davis taking hold of Danion's chair.

"Don't!" she said popping her head up.

"As I said..." he told Danion. "She's fine."

As Davis stepped away from Danion Jordan struggled to pull Danion's chair back into the shadows away from the approaching sunlight that was entering the room when it suddenly occurred to her that Davis knew something that he shouldn't.

"Boyfriend?" she said looking at Danion who then looked at Davis.

"Yes…and let me tell you I was amazed. A werewolf and a vampire...but I've seen stranger things."

"How?" Jordan asked.

"He had me followed since I got here…maybe before." said Danion.

"Not exactly." Davis corrected him. "I started having you followed the day she broke into the house. Alone in a room with a Howler and you come out untouched. At first I thought she was a member of the Consortia… imagine my surprise when I found out otherwise. Now what's a Howler doing with the Gur-Fanng?"

"Why's a Drac-cul pretending to be a Daisy?" she said.

"So, you figured out my little secret?" said Davis. "Such cleverness should be rewarded."

He snapped his fingers and James came into the room holding a tray of food.

"I obviously had to give the housekeeper the day off but perhaps you just might survive James's culinary arts." Davis said.

"I think you'll like this." James said showing a cut up apple, banana, and a bowl of dry cereal.

Davis looked and answered.

"Well...you thought wrong." said Davis knocking the tray from James's hands. "Now go get something to clean this mess with and do take your time. The more you're away from me the better I like it."

James hurried off to clean up the mess that Davis made without hesitation or objection.

"Now…where were we?" asked Davis. "Ooh…yes. James and me."

Davis told them that he found James on the street when he was fourteen. One look at him and Davis knew that James was as easily controlled mind. At first, he was going to make James his Daywatcher since he hadn't had one in a long time but then realized he could be used in better ways than just a lackey. So a plan began to build a corporate empire with James as a puppet king and Davis pulling the strings. Using mind control to put the words in James's mouth, Davis constantly belittling himself through James to better keeps his cover as James's lap-dog finance man. This way he had full access to the corporate accounts and could make money decisions without anyone batting an eye. That was only the first part of his brilliant plan. Davis to hide himself even better in the background decided to plant the idea to anyone or thing that James was more than he seemed. In that he kept James out of the public eye for years. Gave him a past with suspicious holes in it. And of course, a good plastic surgeon to maintain a preserved look. With that all curious eyes would be on James while Davis was free to move.

"Good plan." Danion said. "So, when did you find out about the flex?"

"A couple of years ago. Of course, I thought it was a nexus at the time. It wasn't till now I was able to move on it. Admittedly the nexus being a flex is a new wrinkle but without the threat of the Consortia looming over me it's a small matter of adjustment." Davis said confidently.

"They're gonna find out." said Jordan.

"She's right…we've already made sure that the Consortia finds out about the flex." said Danion.

"I'm assuming this is your little plan to get the Elders to tell your little Consortia partner about the flex thus calling in the Consortia themselves?" Davis asked in a calm and unworried matter. "Sorry…but that's not going to happen. Actually…I'm not really sorry at all."

Both Danion and Jordan looked at each other with equal expressions of 'How did he know?' with Danion asking "Why won't it happen?"

"Because I'm not going to tell them." Lee-Shannon said flying into the room to sit on top of Davis's shoulder.

"What the…?" Danion said staring at her perplexed. "Are you fucking kiddin' me?!"

"Danion...?" Jordan asked knowing this was not good.

"She's the one the Consortia sent." Danion said. "The one who was---"

"...Supposed to get the Elders to curse James." said Davis finishing Danion's sentence. "Yes, I know. I can see you are somewhat confused by this…maybe I should explain."

Davis knew for a long time that the Consortia had plans for James and his business, meaning Davis's

business, thanks to his informant Lee-Shannon. But he was never able to find out exactly what it was and thus wasn't able to defend himself against it.

"You got a mole inside the Consortia?" Danion said with amazement.

"A difficult feat to achieve but luckily she was already a member of the Consortia which made things much easier." said Davis. "Now again...where was I?"

Davis continued by saying when he decided to make his move on the flex he wanted everyone to think he wanted the land and the land alone. This worked perfectly because Davis knew that the Consortia wouldn't help the OC. Their job was primarily keeping the Lore a secret and not stopping land grabs. Also, that the OC Elders wouldn't call for the Consortia because they could discover the flex and take it away from them. Of course, there was always the possibility the OC would call the Consortia and use the flex as a motivator, or that the Consortia would send an agent to make sure the OC and the Gur-Fanng efforts to keep their land didn't expose the Lore and inadvertently discover the flex themselves.

So, how to keep the flex a secret from the Consortia, especially with a spy in his mitts. Oddly enough the answer came to Davis when he found out the Consortia's plans to get James cursed by the OC for stealing their land thanks to Lee-Shannon. Now a plan was in focus. Complex and difficult but if it worked it would ensure Davis getting the land, the Consortia's ignorance of what was on the land, and expose the hidden plans the Consortia had for James Industries. Actually…it wasn't complex as you think. All Davis had to do was sit back and watch Danion get the land from the OC as order by the Consortia. Then Lee-Shannon would convince the Elders to curse James. Danion would then 'suggest' the help of the Consortia to free James from the curse. They would remove the curse but not without putting a price-tag for that help. James would have no choice but to agree while in truth Davis would secretly get the curse removed from James before the Consortia showed up with their price-tag still thinking that James was cursed. The Consortia would think they have the upper-hand when in fact Davis through James would maneuver things to work best for him.

You see…simple. If you hang upside down with you back to a mirror and one eye wide shut.

"So…any questions?" Davis asked as if he just gave a collage lecture.

"No…sounds like a great plan." Danion said in false praise of Davis.

"Yes, it is." said Davis. "I do admit there were some surprises that I didn't count on. The OC getting reinforcements. The Gur-Fanng with that damn court order. You."

"Me?" asked Danion.

"When you first came here I saw some reluctance to this job. Then you did a complete turn-around by wanting to hiring trolls to destroy the OC village. 'Couldn't let that happen but of course I couldn't let James say anything to stop you either."

"So, you get Lee-Shannon to do it for you." said Danion. "Why? Wouldn't the trolls speed up your plan.?"

"No…it could have set things back." said Davis.

Okay…Curses 102. A curse can only be placed on a person once at a time and for one reason for that time. Davis could not allow Danion's plan of attacking the OC village to succeed. If a fairie or many fairies would have died there was a chance the OC would use that to curse James. If they did Davis through James would not have gotten the land and he needed the OC to curse James for taking the land. Also…he had a very particular curse he wanted Lee-Shannon to get OC to perform.

"And how exactly were you going to remove the curse without the help of the Consortia?" Danion asked.

A sly grin formed on Davis's face in saying, 'Ooh…you are going feel so stupid for this one'.

"The Surreal." he answered.

Danion closed his eyes and reluctantly nodding his head in acknowledging the Surreal.

"You see Lee-Shannon here has already put herself in the good gracious of the OC and the Elders by telling them about the first and 'second' troll attack. Too bad she 'didn't know' about the kidnapping of the Offspring but you can't know everything." said Davis. "Still…they did take that leap of faith to tell Lee about the flex to get the Consortia to stop me...sorry I meant James. Big mistake."

The plan was to tell the OC that if Lee-Shannon told the Consortia about the flex the Consortia would want the flex more than helping the Offspring and more than likely the OC would lose their land forever. Lee-Shannon however would convince the Elders that she was more loyal to her OC heritage than her Consortia vows. First…they would get the Offspring back by surrendering the land. Then the OC would place a curse on James that would get their land back without the Consortia's knowing about the flex. Once the curse was on James, a particular curse that Davis wanted placed on James, Lee-Shannon would go back to the Consortia telling them it was done and covering herself with them. Davis would then have the curse removed from

James by the Surreal and wait for the Consortia to revive their plans. The OC couldn't blame Lee-Shannon if James used other means than giving back the land to remove their curse and 'knew' that Lee-Shannon was putting her life on the line by not telling the Consortia about the flex, honor demanded they keep silent to protect her.

"Wait…your plan…and the Consortia's plan was me…telling you…that the Consortia could remove the curse. How was that going to happen with you 'killing' me?" asked Danion.

"The Consortia would have found a way to contact James with or without you." Said Davis

Again, Danion acknowledged that.

"So…who shot us?" Jordan asked.

It wasn't really relevant now but she just wanted to know

"A moron who couldn't do the job right." answered Davis looking at the direction of James. "How he could foul the job up with a laser-sighted crossbow and rifle is beyond me. I knew I should had sent Lee to chaperone him."

"So how are you gonna finish the job now?" asked Jordan.

"Now what makes you think I want to do that?" asked Davis.

"Because the bad guy only reveals their master plan to the good guys when he's about to kill them." said Jordan.

"Or asked the good guy to join him." said Davis.

"What?" Danion said.

"My decision to kill you Danion was the right one…I would do it again." Davis said frankly. "I could have killed you both earlier but quickly realized by doing that I was robbing both of us of great opportunities. Even though you were a spy I honestly have to say you have been one of the best employees I have ever worked with…and there have been many. You're effective. Focused. Hell, you're work speaks for itself. London, San Francisco, and most recently Brazil. I don't see why things should change now."

"Because the Consortia would kill me like they're going to kill her for betraying them." Danion said looking at Lee-Shannon.

"Well…that's the thing Danion. The Consortia already thinks you're dead." said Davis.

"Why would---Because you told them I was dead." Danion understood again looking at Lee-Shannon.

"'Seems an elf's arrow found its way to your heart." said Davis

"Walsh was devastated by the news." said Lee-Shannon.

"With the Consortia thinking you're dead you can still work for me. Of course, you'll have to lay low for…ever, but I'll more than compensate you for that inconvenience." said Davis.

"You're serious." realized Danion.

"Quite. Think about it Danion. With the flex in my control nothing will be beyond my grasp." Davis said to Danion. "Not even the imagination."

Danion stared at Davis and knew that he wasn't exaggerating about that statement.

"Hell…I even make room for your little dog." Davis added to Danion looking at Jordan.

"I'm nobody's dog." Jordan pointed out with a growl insulted by the comment.

"Heel your tongue she-wolf." said Davis. "'Bit volatile, isn't she?"

"Call her a dog again and you'll see just how much?" said Danion.

"So…are you in?" Davis asked.

"Do I have a choice?" asked Danion.

"Yes...I kill you." answered Davis. "…and her."

"My...not much of a dilemma there." Danion said looking at Jordan who was wondering how they were going to get out of this one.

Her eyes were clearly shouting, 'Don't trust him!' but she also knew Danion would probably say, 'Yes.' to save her.

"No." he said.

Surprise came from all around the room especially from Jordan.

"Not that I don't appreciate your offer but I think I'll take my chances on the Other Side than what the Consortia would do to me." said Danion.

"And her?" Davis said referring to Jordan.

"I hope we end up in the same place." said Danion looking at Jordan. "So…can we get this over with please. I truly do admit your plan within a plan is brilliant. How you arranged to get Lee-Shannon chosen to be the other agent on this case alone was genius…but it still won't work."

Suddenly Davis and Lee-Shannon started laughing.

"Now that's one of the more amusing parts of this." said Davis. "I didn't 'arrange' for Lee to be made the other agent. They chose her on their own. That's how I found out about the plan in the first place."

"They chose her?" said Danion.

"The irony of it was just too funny." smiled Davis. "Them choosing my mole to trick the OC into cursing James."

"Well…that's a very interesting coincidence." said Danion.

"Oh, I had my suspicions but then I realized the Consortia didn't know about Lee." said Davis.

"You're so sure about that?" asked Danion.

Suddenly there was a stare between Danion and Davis. It shook Davis a little as he saw a tiny smile form around Danion's lips and a minute later the phone rang.

"Excuse me I have to go into lackey mode." said Davis.

He motioned to James who pulled out a gun and pointed it at Jordan.

"Silver bullets." Davis said. "Won't kill you but I pretty sure it won't do her any good. I suggest you stay very, very, quiet."

Feeling he had nothing to fear from Danion or Jordan Davis hit the 'speaker' button on the phone to answer it.

"Derrick James's residence." he said.

The sound of clapping came over the speaker. Everyone had a confused look of 'What the...?" then a voice spoke.

"Truly a brilliant plan Mister Davis." it said.

Danion and Lee-Shannon instantly recognized the voice as Walsh.

"No denying it…absolutely brilliant. All this time and we thought… well I thought. Again, the old saying is true 'It's always the quiet ones'."

"I beg your pardon?" Davis asked with a mix of confusion and fear.

Confusion over what Walsh was talking about and fear that he knew exactly what Walsh was talking about.

"You just confessed all Mister Davis. Please don't insult us both by professing ignorance now." said Walsh. "As for the flex…I'm sure you'll understand we'll be taking custody of that from the OC rather than you."

A blank look came over Davis hearing that announcement. 'How the hell did they find out?' he asked himself. Then the answer became quite clear as he looked over to Danion. With an intensified anger shooting from his eyes Davis backhanded Danion across the face.

"Where is it?" said Davis.

"Where's what?" Danion said.

"The bug!" Davis shouted with another hit across Danion's face. "Where is it?!"

"I think...you just knock it out." Danion said feeling the taste of blood in his mouth.

Davis grabbed Danion by the chin and forced Danion's mouth open looking inside.

He couldn't see anything but he knew where the bug was now.

"A dental mic?" an astonished Davis said.

"A little 'Mission Impossible' I know but hey... it worked." said Danion.

"They've know all the time?" asked Davis.

"About you? No…not till you told them. About Lee-Shannon as James's mole… long time now." said Danion.

"That's why Lee-Shannon was assigned to get the OC to curse James. We knew full well she would warm him...well you." voiced Walsh.

Davis looked over to Lee-Shannon with that same intense stare he gave Danion.

"What did you do wrong?" he said.

"W-What?" Lee-Shannon asked.

"What-Did-You-Do Wrong?" he repeated. "What did you do to tip them off?"

"Nothing." she answered with fear over the anger in Davis's eyes.

"Don't be mad at her." said Danion. "It wasn't the whole Consortia. It was just Walsh at first. He always suspected something after Zarafinn."

Davis's anger seemed to increase with that information.

"You told me there were not going to be any problems from that, Lee-Shannon!"

"He's lying." said Lee-Shannon.

"Is he?" voiced Walsh. "You should have stayed suspicious Davis. Especially since the one who assigned Lee to this mission used to be one of

Zarafinn's past partners. Then again...you probably would have if you knew Danion was another."

"You were partners with Zarafinn?" Lee-Shannon asked Danion.

"For four long years." he answered.

"That means you're..."

Davis couldn't finish the sentence so Danion did it for him with some slight enjoyment.

"A card-carrying member of the Consortia." he said.

Danion looked over to Jordan who was staring at him over this new information. As their eyes locked there was a sudden understanding about it all. She now knew what Danion was holding back from her. The reason why he wanted to marry her and wouldn't. He was a member of the Consortia and the complexities of that were ooh...so clear. Then just as suddenly their moment of understanding was shattered by Davis taking the gun out of James's hands and putting a bullet into Danion that knocked him backward to the ground from the impact.

"Danion!" Walsh yelled over the phone hearing the gunshot.

The response was a bullet destroying the phone.

"You-stupid-insect!!" Davis yelled pinning Lee-Shannon against the wall with the barrel of the gun that was like a cannon up against her small fairie body.

"Since when do Lore use guns?" Jordan yelled at Davis.

Her statement wasn't to save Lee-Shannon but to keep Davis from putting another bullet in Danion or herself. She hoped a reminder of Lore pride would do that.

She was wrong.

"My dear…I have survived the centuries by adapting to the times and abandoning the ways that can get me killed." said Davis. "But if it makes you feel better..."

Davis lowered the gun making Lee-Shannon breathe a sigh of relief only to have widened eyes at the sight of a letter opener slicing into her. If she hadn't moved just the slightest bit she would have been cut in half. Instead she fell to the floor holding on to her side trying to keep her insides inside.

"You don't have time to kill her Davis." said Danion.

"I'll make the time." said Davis.

"By now the Consortia has already sent someone to take the flex and deal with the OC, Gur-Fanng, and more than likely you." said Danion. "Now you may be a Drac-cul but not even you can take on the Consortia...especially during the day."

"The daylight. The one weakness to all vampires." said Davis. "For most... fatal."

With that one statement Danion and Jordan knew what was on Davis's mind as he looked towards the glass doors to the bright sunlight outside.

"You could do that but what would be the point?" said Danion.

"No point at all…except spite." Davis said picking up a still tied up Danion and throwing him through the sliding glass doors.

Glass shattered everywhere as Danion landed outside in the full view of the daylight. He immediately felt the heat of sun rays hitting his skin then the heat of the flames as his skin caught on fire.

Jordan didn't need enhance hearing for Danion's shouts of pain to echo through her ears. The situation was made even more painful as Jordan was chained in place keeping her from helping Danion.

"Don't worry…it will be over soon." he said.

"Let me go!" she cried with yellow eyes.

"No." Davis said as if the answer wasn't obvious.

Not even in full were mode could Jordan break free from her chains. Reverting back into human form she suddenly remembered what I said about a Vam-wolf having more strength than a werewolf and vampire combined. The first time with Grull it was in a panic without her realizing it but now she was trying to summon it up with no effect.

Then she noticed that Danion's shouts had stopped replaced with silence and the smell of something burning outside.

"No. No! **Nooo!!**" she screamed again going into full werewolf mode this time with the added feature of glowing red eyes.

Like they say, 'A chain is only as strong as its' weakest link.' which broke apart freeing Jordan to attack Davis. Davis himself was caught off guard by her breaking the chains. The surprise was doubled when Jordan backhanded Davis with a blow that sent him flying across the room.

Her first instinct was to help Danion but as she got to the edge of the sliding glass doors she had a panic attack causing her to go back into human form. Her mind flashbacked to that hotel room in Denver and that pile of dust she thought was Danion. Instantly those emotions came flooding back as if it was happening for the first time and the thought of going through that again paralyzed her. She couldn't go outside and see another pile of dust.

She just couldn't.

Unfortunately...this gave Davis more than enough time to recover and throw Jordan against another wall. He then pulled the classic move of picking her up by the throat with one hand and choking the life out of her. She tried once again to use that extra Vam-wolf strength but it wasn't happening again.

"I may have lost the flex. I may be exposed to the Consortia...but I can always start over. You will not have that luxury." he said "It would be sooo easy just to put a bullet in your brain but I must confess...I simply just enjoy watching the life go out in one's eyes."

"Then...you're really going to be disappointed today." said Danion.

Davis turned his head with shocked eyes only to have them grow wider at the sight of Danion standing at the sliding glass doorway with the sun shining brightly behind him. His skin had patches of second degree burns from sun exposure but of course it was better than complete disintegration.

"Impossible...How...?" Davis asked with an opened mouth of astonishment and disbelief.

"I guess...I owe a mad scientist an apology." said Danion. "Put her down...Now!"

"No." Davis said in a tone as if it was ridiculous that Danion was giving him orders.

"Yes." Danion said grabbing James by the throat and choking him. "Or your little puppet loses his head."

"And...?" asked Davis.

It was a useless threat. They both knew Davis had no need for James anymore but that didn't mean that Danion couldn't use James for something else. Like throwing him at Davis. Davis swatted James out of the air like a fly giving Danion the distraction to make a flying charge at Davis forcing him to let go of Jordan. He slammed Davis against the wall, something that usually wouldn't even phase Davis, but it was daytime.

Now…why is that so important you asked?

Though Drac-cul can survive daylight it's still their worst enemy because it extremely weakens them. Their transmutation powers are gone. Their mind-control is so low that they have to be at close range to their puppets. And most importantly their strength is cut in half. A Drac-cul has the strength of about 20 to 25 men at night while a House vampire has about the strength of 8 to 10. Good news is that a House doesn't lose their strength in the daylight hours. Add the power of a werewolf to the mix and you have someone who could take a Drac-cul...at least during the daytime.

The two of them started knocking each other around the room. Into the walls, the floor, and furniture. Somehow Davis got the upper-hand and put Danion into some police like neck-hold. Danion responded by flying straight up and positioning his body so that Davis would ram right into the ceiling. It made Davis loosen his hold so Danion started spinning in the air like a top to fling Davis off him. Davis landed on his back but quickly recovered to get to his feet and looked up at Danion to decide his next move. That's when Davis felt the tightness of the chain wrapping around his neck. Before he could do anything Jordan in full werewolf mode flipped Davis over her and planted him on the floor. She did it a second time and then a third. 'Can't really tell you when she stopped but by the time she did Davis was thoroughly softened up with bruises, blood, and a possible slipped disc. Danion then picked up Davis and was about to land one serious power fist to the center of Davis's face when he noticed that his punch would send Davis through the already shattered glass doors. So he carefully positioned Davis a little to the left and then landed his punch sending Davis outside the house through the wall.

"Petty revenge." Danion said to Jordan. "Sue me."

A snicker from Jordan told him she wasn't complaining.

Davis was truly feeling the pain now. He looked back at the house and the hole he went through and did not want to go another round with Danion and Jordan knowing he couldn't take them…at least not now. Davis looked as the two walked out on the patio and watched perplexed and relieved as Danion was forced back inside by the sun that once again setting his skin on fire.

Danion yelled out as Jordan helped put the flames out on him. Davis seeing this used the opportunity to pull out a second cell-phone and punch in a few numbers.

"'Can't take the heat Danion?" he said staggering up to his feet. "What a shame. It's such a beautiful day."

His taunting of Danion made Jordan start to move outside but Danion grabbed her arm to stop her.

"No." he said.

"But I can get him." said Jordan.

"No. The Sun. Sage was right. I could take it but it didn't last." he said showing the freshly burned skin on his hand. "There's no telling what it could do to you now."

Jordan looked outside to the light and quickly passed her claw through it. No burns but she could feel an uncomfortable heat from the sun making her wary to venture outside but no less determined to finish off Davis who she saw hobbling towards the woods.

"He's getting away." she growled.

"Let him."

"But he knows where the Offspring are."

"And I'm betting so do they." said Danion looking over to an unconscious James and a nearly bleeding to death Lee-Shannon. "See if you can wake James up…I really doubt Lee-Shannon's in the mood for speaking now."

Going back to human form Jordan starting slapping James back into consciousness.

"Wake-up. Wake-up! Where are the Offspring?" she yelled.

"W-Where's the master? I can't feel him anymore." said James.

"Your master…"

"Is dead." Danion announced to James. "If you don't want to join him you will tell us where the Offspring are."

"No…he is eternal. He lives. He will come for me and I will never betray him." said James.

A laugh came out of Danion over what was in front him. For two years he believed James to be a corporate genius and possible Lore. Now he was a groveling lap-dog one step above a slave. Either way Jordan didn't like James's lack of assistance.

"Maybe keeping your heart in your chest will make you change your mind." she said morphing her hand back into a claw and sticking the sharpened fingernails in James's chest.

Needless to say there was a lot of pain going through James's body until Danion pulled Jordan's clawed nails out of James's chest.

"'Better idea…" he said to her. "James…I need you to tell me where the Offspring are...now."

James looked into Danion's eyes and felt a slight headache as his mind was being controlled to give up the location of the Elder Offspring. The info didn't even take five seconds to get as James gave up the secret like a reality show.

"There's a landline in the kitchen" Danion told Jordan. "Call the Gur-Fanng and get the Offspring."

"Right." she said and did…right after she knocked James unconscious again with a closed fist.

The moment that Jordan was gone, Danion went over to Lee-Shannon, who was semi-conscious herself to hear what Danion was saying.

"Take my advice." he said to her. "Die now. It will be a lot better than what the Consortia will do to you."

When Jordan returned she had this perplexed/gleeful look on her face that made Danion worry about what was happening.

"What's wrong? You couldn't get to the Gur-Fanng?" he asked.

"No…I got to them."

"So there gonna get the Offspring?"

"They…already have 'em." she said.

"What? How?"

"I don't know…they got some sorta tip. Fought some trolls. Got the Offspring"

"And the Major?"

"I don't know I didn't ask. But who cares…we've won!"

"Against Davis but now you're going to have to deal with the Consortia over the flex. Well at least the OC does."

"The Consortia??" She asked.

By the tone of her voice Danion knew where things were going to go next.

"How---?"

"If you're going to ask me the question I know you're going to ask me then I would think you would already know the answer." said Danion.

"Yeah…the almighty Consortia." she scoffed. "You've been lying since day one."

"Yes…I've lied about a few things." he confessed. "But only to protect you."

"From what?"

"From them." said Danion. "I don't want them knowing about you."

"Well…it's a little late with that mouth radio broadcasting everything." she said

"I can turn it off and on anytime I want and it was always off when we were together."

"Well…they had to found out when Davis spouted his guts over his brilliant plan."

"It was Walsh's idea for the dental mic. Only he and I knew about it so only he…I hope…was listening in. Him I trust. So I'm pretty sure the Consortia won't find out about you." he said.

"Why are you scared that the Consortia will find out about me?"

"Because the Consortia will use anything to keep their agents in line." he said. "I'm known as a bit of a rogue in the ranks. Mainly because they don't have anything to use against me....at least they didn't." he said looking at her

A long silence came between them as Danion stepped closer her. She knew what he was going to say and he knew that she knew what she was going to say but he said it anyway.

"Go home Jordan. Live a long and happy life." he said to her. "And with all the blessing in the world get married. You will make a beautiful bride...to someone who can say, 'I do'."

He turned away from her so Jordan wouldn't see the pain in his eyes over letting go of the one woman he loved again. She watched as he started to walk away and knew why he said what he did. It was in his voice especially when he talked about her getting married and the sadness she felt from him. No matter how he tried to hide it he knew that he was not going to be the one to say 'I do'. He loved her. There was no doubt about it just like in Denver and because of it Jordan also knew there was no way in hell she was going to let that love go so easily.

The next thing that happened was Danion feeling the pain of Jordan smashing a chair across his back. As he fell to the floor she took his head and started slamming his face against the floor. She then turned him over and sat on his chest while grabbing his collar to give him the facts on her and him.

"Listen to me you sonvabitch we are getting married!" she said. "You are not leaving me again. You try and I will hunt you down and will rip the skin off your body. Do you understand me?!"

"It may take a while…my head's still ringing." Danion laughed with pain.

"Shut-up! I don't care if you're a part of the Consortia, I don't care what you've done with them, and I don't give a damn if they know about me! We are getting married and no one is going to stop us!" she shouted into his mouth so whoever might be listening would hear her loud and clear.

"I turned it off you're only yelling at me."

"uh...good. 'Cause what I'm gonna say next is just between you and me."

"That being?" he asked.

"Hello?" she said as if it wasn't obvious. "The Vam-wolf thing... It's real now. I don't know what I'm in for here. I don't know about you but I'm a... I'm more than a little freaked out and I don't plan on going through that alone. Besides...do you really wanna be anywhere near the Consortia if they find out you can walk in the sun?"

Danion paused to think about it.

"No...not really." he answered.

"Thought so. So staying together would probably be a pretty good idea right now."

She reached into her pocket and pulled out her bracelet from Danion.

"This is gonna be my engagement ring." she said showing it to him. "Once I put it on it's done."

"It's done? Oh...I feel soo romanced Mrs. Jordan."

"Rail."

"What?"

"Rail." she repeated. "It... feels so much better when you call me Rail."

"Then I guess pet names are out of the question huh?"

"Call me 'Pookie' and the ripping of skin is immediate." she said.

"I'll stick with Rail."

"You bet you will."

A smile formed on Rail's face as she put her bracelet back on her right wrist over her bracelet tattoo. After so long it felt soo good to have it back especially knowing what it meant for her and Danion's future. She stared at it with the expressions of a 'bride to be' then noticed something she didn't before.

"Why is it a little melted here?" she asked showing him.

"Demon blood..." the kid said. "Don't ask."

"Well that's it. Whatever happens…happens. Let it come…we'll deal with it..." Rail said helping Danion to his feet. "...Together."

"Good…because there's going to be a lot of things coming our way." he said thinking about their future.

"You don't know the half it." she said thinking about her past.

And with that the suspense was...well nearly over. It was 'done'. Danion and Rail were finally engaged.

God help us all.

Now I know what you're thinking, 'What happened to Davis?'. I would tell you but right then I was too busy trying to keep him from choking me to death. You see I got worried about Danion and Rail when dawn passed and there was no word from them. I went through the woods thinking I would sneak up on things unnoticed. Big mistakes since I ran smack-damb into Davis, and of course with what always happens to me in these situations, I found myself pinned against something…namely a tree, off my feet, (and this part is really gotten redundant…) by the throat. But no worries. I had everything under control…as I was screaming like a five-year-old child. Things didn't get better when Davis got a look at me.

A good look.

A really good look.

"You!" he said tightening his grip on my throat.

"Okay…I'm guessing you're still a little angry about the Rome thing."

"I-am-going-to-kill-you."

"Uhh, you could do that, true, but I much prefer sitting down and having some frozen yogurt."

"Still the funny man. Well…I guess after all this time I'll be getting the last laugh." he smiled still increasing his grip.

Right there Davis started getting a massive headache. The pain was like his head was splitting open with only seconds before his brain would explode. He let go of me and stumbled backwards holding his head.

"Sorry to disappoint you." I said a little horsed but then I thought about it. "No...not really. Obviously, you've had a bad day...or century. I can understand that but have some faith...with my compliments."

Again, the pain went shearing through Davis's head. Usually you don't see that sort of behavior in a Drac-cul unless they're face to face with the Holy Cross. Of course, everybody knows that it's not the cross that does the trick but the faith behind it. You see faith works on a psi level that can be used against Drac-cul but most people can't generate the necessary brain power for it to be effective. So, they need a focal point, something to believe in and put their will power through to stop a Drac-cul...namely the Cross. Doesn't need to be a cross to do the job. Anything will work as long as you have your faith behind it...and sometimes when your mind and will are strong enough faith is all you need.

Hey, I've said it before...I have my moments.

"I would ask why you're here but seeing you makes it pretty clear. Davis...right? You mind-screwed some poor bastard into your puppet to gain power then controlled that power from behind the scenes. One would think you would use a new M.O. since the last time went soo 'well'."

"Ooh…I should have known you were a part of this somehow. Wait…mad scientist." he realized. "No…not again. I am not losing to you again."

He tried to charge at me but another dose of faith drove him back.

"You were always a sore loser, Gus. Real glad we got the Elder Offspring away from the Major and those trolls. Being from old Rome you probably would have ordered their deaths as some form of petty spite.

"How did you know where to find them?" he asked.

"Well…I know a lot more than I did before."

Davis, who I knew as 'Gus' some time ago, eyes widened as he realized the meaning behind my statement.

"You...found it…didn't you? You found it!"

"No…it found me." I said. "And let me tell you the union has not been a joyous one. It's a miracle it told me where the Offspring were because it never tells you what you need to know. Tells you what you want to know but never what you need to know. 'Pot at the end of the rainbow' sure… it just leaves out the part that it's protected by man-eating leprechauns, but I 'digest', weren't you leaving?"

"This is not over. I'll be---"

"I'll be back. I'll have my revenge. I shall suffer the consequences. La-la-la-bla. Get in line behind Dana, 109, and an old werewolf grandmother." I said. "But remember…I already own all the media rights to this entire story."

"So…you are responsible for those two freaks back there." said Davis.

"Danion and Rail? Kicked your ass, huh? No…I was just as surprised by that as I'm sure you were." I said noticing Davis's bruises. "Y'know it told me if I came up here I would find something that no one has seen in a 1000-years. At first, I thought it was...nevermind. But if it's them it's not the dawn of the Vam-wolf…it's the return. Ooh future developments should be…quite interesting."

"Yes...quite interesting indeed." Davis said in a tone that expressed an interest that I didn't like.

"Are you still here?" I said to him ready to give him another blast of faith.

"I'm going." he said quickly stepping back into the woods.

"Here's to never seeing each other ever again, Gus." I said to him in a mock toast.

"Well, we can only hope...'Vince'."

And with that Davis disappeared into woods never to be seen again.

Oh, please I read way too many comic books to know that wasn't going to happen.

Okay…so now we're in the final stretch where we tie up all… well, most of the loose ends of our story. The Consortia came to Jackson Point like clockwork and confronted the Elders about the flex surprisingly letting them keep it. They kept the secret this long so why not let them keep up the good work. Of course the Consortia wanted monthly reports from the Elders to make sure it was still a secret.

They looked for Davis but he had disappeared along with all the money that was James Industries. The corporate grapevine was buzzing over how James was broke in a heartbeat but things were all cleared up when the money all reappeared thanks to the Consortia. This gave them yet another foothold in the corporate world and as for James he was under Davis's control for so long he couldn't function on his own. Luckily…he had a new 'Finance adviser' who told him building on the OC land wasn't very cost effective and to move on to more profitable enterprises. She's very good at her job and always stays close to James.

Except outside in the daylight.

Though the OC were safe from any more land grabs, they themselves were not happy that one of their own had betrayed them, the same went for the Consortia. It was decided the OC would carry out Lee-Shannon's punishment. It seemed to be a fair and right move by the Consortia for their part in trying to help James/Davis steal their land… which they still had not mention to the OC. Lee-Shannon may have survived that letter-opener but how would she do from being near immortal and able to fly to being just plain human. A curse was finally placed by the Elders and let me tell you… life for a human with no money, ID, and no one to help is well...shitty. I knew someone who went through the same thing. Now that was a time...I miss her.

Craig Matters? Well…he got much the admiration from both the OC and the Gur-Fanng when he led the rescue mission to free the Offspring. Many a young female shined an eye towards Craig for his heroism…one of them not surprisingly being Kefflynn.

A werewolf and a Fairie?

Stranger unions have happened.

Now, I'm sure you have more questions but ask me later. I have a multitude of strip joints to check out for Danion's future bachelor party for…'Research'. I'm hoping for the title of best man that's why Carla and I are heading south to New Orleans. I heard about a little...'Social club' who's employees cater to the 'unusual'.

Should be a good time.

Even better if they don't let you take pictures.

What?

You think I forgotten about Danion and Rail.

No way.

They took off before the Consortia showed up leaving Rail's 'Good-byes' to her Jackson Point family to quick phone calls and later hand-written letters. Their leaving was attempt to get a head start from the Consortia and learn more about the Vam-wolf in them.

Danion eventually knew he had to go back to the Consortia. What worried him was how they would react when they discover he was a new species of Lore. More importantly he didn't know how he and Rail were going to protect themselves if the Consortia didn't look favorably on this new species.

I told the kid not to worry and I'll be back in a few days...or weeks. Good research takes time…and we can meet up in a safe place and I'll start running tests to see what effects the merging of the two ancient enemies had on them. Danion wasn't too happy about that and he wanted answers now.

Understandable but I really needed to get to the 'Big Easy' so I gave him a little pre-wedding gift to calm his anxiety

What gift?

Wait and see.

The sun shined brightly over the cabin house where Danion and Rail were staying. Rail came outside and felt the rays hit her skin. It was still mildly uncomfortable but I was working on a sunscreen to fix that.

"Come on." she said trying to coach Danion to come outside into the light.

"The first time could have been a fluke." he said staying in the shaded protection of the front porch.

"A fluke, huh? Flukes happen once." she said. "I've been able to do this for a week."

She closed her eyes and almost immediately started rising off the ground. She was less than three feet in the air when she looked over to Danion and smiled. Then she decided to show off by spinning backward like a carnival ride.

"Very good." he said clapping his hands. "But I'll really be impressed once you can get more than two feet off the ground."

She stopped spinning and made a face at him not watching her footing when she came back to earth and landing on her ass.

"And your landing could use a little work." he laughed.

"Ha-ha." she said not seeing the humor and holding out her hand for Danion to help her up.

He looked at her in saying 'The sun's still out'. She looked at him in saying 'You'll be fine' again trying to coach him out. Danion wasn't willing to take the chance by his facial expression and Rail responded with her own facial expression of 'Get your ass out here!'

He slowly stuck his hand out in the sunlight and braced himself for the pain. There was none. It was bit uncomfortable from the heat but no smoke, fire, or burning. So...with on firm motion he pushed himself fully out into the sunlight. He looked up to the sun and felt it's warm rays wash over his body.

"So, how long has it been?" Rail asked seeing Danion standing in a place he thought he never be in again.

"A very long time." he said taking her hand.

As he helped her up she looked at him with a goofy smile on her face about the realization of things.

"What?" he asked seeing that smile.

"We're really getting married."

"If I want to keep the skin on my body, yeah."

"Come on..." she playfully hitting him on his shoulder. "Married. As in Mr. and Mrs.... Uhh? Mr. and Mrs. What?"

"Sorry?"

"Your last name? Mr. and Mrs....?"

"I don't know. I never had one in the first place and when I was 'Bought over' I kept changing my last name like everybody else."

"Well get one 'cause I'm gonna be Mrs....'Somebody'."

"Let's just use your last name." he said.

"It's not the same."

The tone in her voice said that this was really important to her. Danion wanted to know 'why?' but Rail rolled her eyes feeling stupid. There was a reason but it was a 'girl' reason and she didn't want Danion to see her acting like a 'girl'.

Then she decided she didn't care.

"I wanna be called Mrs." she said a little embarrassed. "It's stupid but it's official when you're called Mrs...'Somebody'. Everybody knows you're married and I want everyone to know we're married…that I'm your wife and you're my husband."

Danion looked at his bride to be and knew no one in love would think that was a stupid reason for having a last name.

"Cooper." he said to her. "How do you like that as a last name.?"

"Not a lot." she answered.

She may have been happy Danion was choosing a last name for her to go by Mrs… but that was not going to be it.

"Okay…how 'bout Powell?" he said.

"No way."

"Stewart?"

"Stewart?... Aren't those all those old black and white movie star names." she asked.

"So?" he said not seeing a problem.

"Ooh you are not naming yourself after some old actor from the last century."

"Hey…my last name…my choice."

"I'm taking your last name…choose better."

"I don't believe this…you ask me to make a decision then you hate the decision I make. It's like we're already married."

There was a small silence between them then they started giggling at each other because this is what married people do. Then Rail's smiled slightly disappeared as her mind flashbacked to something.

"What?" Danion asked.

"Nothing." she said trying to ignore it.

"What?" he wanted her to tell him.

"It's... just that when I little my grandma always wanted to plan my wedding." she said feeling like a 'girl' again.

"Then we should let her." said Danion.

"I don't know...I'm still angry."

"What's the problem? I'm half werewolf now."

"And I'm half vampire." she worried.

"But she's still your grandmother."

"I gotta think about it."

"Well...who else are we going to invite?"

Danion meant that as incentive for Rail to call her grandmother then she realized who else they could invite.

"Sal...she can be my 'Maid of Honor'."

"Sage's been hinting about 'Best Man'." said Danion. "And I personally would love to deliver the news to Price and Phil-el."

"Oh, that bitch is soo mine." Rail said emphasizing it with yellow werewolf eyes.

"Fine…she's your wedding present." he said. "Maybe by then I'll find a last name you'll like."

"I hope so."

"Hey there are a lot worse names to have than that of classic American film stars."

"Like what?" she laughed thinking that wasn't possible.

"Off the top of my head..." he said with a grin that could barely contain itself. "How 'bout...Calliope."

"Oh…dear god no." Rail said closing her eyes in shame.

She then looked at Danion with the expression screaming, 'How? How the Hell?'.

Danion didn't give up an answer which I'm really grateful for as he ran off laughing with Rail in hot pursuit…determined to find out how he discovered her real name.

Once about a time a werewolf and a vampire fell in love.

After a great adventure and wonderful courtship... treachery and betrayal made each believe the other was dead.

Twelve years later they found each other again and became something that could only exist in a fairy tale.

Though many obstacles still laid ahead of them

(The Consortia, The Quinns, 109, and sadly their own brethren)

All in all...

In the very end...

They did live...

(all together now)

Happily ever after.

AFTERWORDS

So here we are again and thank you for sticking around to read the end of this little trilogy of Danion and Rail. The story is not over it's just put aside for the moment so I can explore other stories outside the C&SB universe.

As for this story… like I said it was to impress the girl but the characters themselves came from a story I thought up about a group of supernatural beings and a vampire and a werewolf were a part of the group. Then I thought what if they were a couple, a werewolf and a vampire dating now there's some drama.

Though I didn't have names for them yet it was Danion who was going to be the werewolf and Rail the vampire, but as I thought about it a werewolf's emotions are more primal and more out there for the world to see and I just simply felt a woman would express that more than a male.

Now… why all the tattoos, piercings, and two strong highlights? I always liked the term 'opposites attract', while Rail would easily fit in at underground garage band rave, Danion if he wasn't so aloof would probably just be another face in the crowd at a California bookstores or coffeehouse. The fact that they were also a mixed raced couple was not a subtle metaphor.

Let's face it in this big old world of ours most of the time the odds are stacked against us. We are not owed anything and the world takes great pleasure in letting us know that little fact. Quite honestly… the world probably doesn't even notice what happens in our little lives, so if you can find someone who can make your life happy does it really matter who they are where they come from?

Of course, I can't condone a person or persons who lie, cheat, and manipulate the world around them to get their happiness. Those individuals may get what they want yet rarely get what they expect and often will get what they deserve.

Thankfully Danion and Rail's relationship started off with something more respectable… a gang fight. Werewolves and vampires, two of the oldest supernatural creatures who hate each other. Why? I tried to find out and the reasons are as wide spread as to why different cultures around the world hate each other but come on… for a writer conflict makes good drama.

There was no way I was not going to write about that for it was the main theme of the storyline but I didn't want it to be all consuming. The first book touched on that issue. The second focused on it and the third had so much other drama happening that that drama wasn't relevant. Which honestly shouldn't be relevant in the real world but there are those who will always make it relevant for the usual reasons and the personal ones.

I wanted to show what two people would do for love. Though I would never recommend setting yourself on fire or waiting for a gunman to put a bullet in your head to see if someone really loves you and I definitely would not recommend a 'no explanation' note no matter how good the intentions.

I'm the last person to give advice on what to do or what not to do in a relationship, each one is different and as much as two people want to be with each together sometimes love is not always enough. It often takes other things… one of those things being honesty. If Danion and Rail were honest with each other at critical points of their relationship there would have been a lot less drama in their lives…of course that would also make less of a story. It was only after they went through the drama that they were honest with one another and things got somewhat better but why does it take so long to get to that point?

In writing the reasons are simple. In real life the reasons are much more complicated but fear has got to be one of the top three. Why? The reasons for that probably outnumber the seconds of the day because there are so many people with equal amount of reasons of why they can't be honest with the one they care about… but are those reasons ever good enough to risk losing the one you love?

Sooner or later you are going to have to overcome that fear, because love is worth it and if it's a good love that two people are willing to be honest and both fight for…it's more than worth it.

Frank Webb.

Made in the USA
Coppell, TX
10 February 2026

71719790R00177